SPELL

PARANORMAL CRI/

LAURA GREENWOOD

CONTENTS

lauragreenwood@authorlauragreenwood.co.uk.
Visit Laura Greenwood's website at:

www.authorlauragreenwood.co.uk
www.facebook.com/authorlauragreenwood/

Cover Design by Logan Keys @ Cover of Darkness
Formatting by Gina Wynn @ Gina Formats Words

Spell Caster is a work of fiction. Names, characters, places, and incidents are the products of the author's imagination or are used fictitiously. Any resemblance to actual persons, living or dead, businesses, companies, events, or locales is entirely coincidental.

BLURB

Can magic and science come together to catch a murderer?

Cassie's world is turned upside down when she's given an unusual blood sample to test. And when a mysterious man shows up at her lab telling her he has the answers she's looking for, she's pulled into a world of murder, investigations, and intrigue.

Finally able to explore the connection between her powers as a witch and her expertise as a scientist to uncover why paranormals keep turning up dead.

ONE

Cassie tightened the band around her hair, trying to hold back the urge to change its colour again. It would be as easy as a single flick of the wrist, but she didn't want to draw too much attention to herself and alert her colleagues that magic was real.

"Cassie?" her boss called.

She turned, her white lab coat swirling with her. "Yes?"

"I have a sample for you, but it's causing a few problems."

She frowned, not sure what to make of that. She trusted her boss, but this sounded almost as if it was off the books, which was a little out of character for him.

"Problems like...?" she prompted.

"It's not going through any of the machines quite right," he replied.

"Is there a chance they're broken?"

He shook his head. "No. I've tried every machine in the building."

"What makes you think I can sort it?" In all likelihood, she could, but she wasn't going to admit that to him just yet. It might raise questions as to how she managed that, and magic wasn't going to be an acceptable answer.

"You're the best technician we have. So far you've managed to get to the bottom of everything we throw at you." He raked his hand through his greying hair, a sheepish grin on his face. "Will you try this one for us?"

Cassie sighed. She really shouldn't. Not if it had failed every machine already. That would just be asking for trouble when she did manage to work it out. And she would. If there was one thing she loved, it was putting different pieces of the puzzle together and discovering the truth of the matter.

"Sure, I'll have a look." The words tumbled out before she could stop them. "But no promises," she added hastily, hoping it was enough to cover her back.

"Thanks, Cassie, you're the best."

That was odd. He never spoke to any of the staff that way. Even if they were doing him a favour and getting to the bottom of mysteries.

"What's the sample code?" Grabbing one of her post-it notes and a pencil, she readied herself to jot it down.

"E6-34U," her boss, Michael, recited.

"Thanks." She flashed him a reserved smile, hoping it'd let him know she wanted to be left alone now.

"Thank you, Cassie. I look forward to hearing what you think." He turned away before she could fully process what he'd just said, but the sense of oddness didn't leave with him.

"Oh well, at least it's a challenge," she muttered to herself, setting aside what she was currently working on and preparing her station to check out the mystery sample.

If she was honest with herself, she was a little bored with this job. There wasn't that much to actually get her mind racing anymore. But it paid well and the hours were good, which was more than she could expect anywhere else given how young she was.

With her workspace cleared, she got out another sheet of paper for her notes, putting the sample number at the top for easy reference. She considered adding about how odd Michael's behaviour was but thought better of it. For now, anyone stopping by her desk would be able to see her notes, and she didn't want to risk them seeing it.

But she would still keep it in mind. It hadn't been right, and that, added to the sample itself, was enough to have her suspicious.

The samples fridge was full to the brim, as always, but she found what she wanted with ease. She lifted the single tray filled with vials carefully, examining it as closely as she dared without knowing if it was poison.

Setting them down on her desk, she grabbed a pair of disposable gloves and snapped them on. It was important she didn't contaminate the sample, mainly so it didn't come up with all the indicators of it belonging to a witch. The last thing she wanted was to be discovered for what she was by accident.

She pulled up a list of the various tests they could do, trying to decide the best way to start the process. She suspected that some of the problem Michael was facing was that the blood belonged to a paranormal and the machines couldn't work out what it was for that exact reason. She almost hoped that was the case, then she could make up some kind of excuses and fake paperwork for it. But something deep down told her there was going to be some other difference that wasn't as easily hidden as the mere existence of paranormals.

It really couldn't be that easy. She'd seen paranormal blood come through before and it had never caused too much of an issue. Especially the types that were mostly human. They just passed through the machine like normal human blood would.

That wasn't why the Witch Council had placed her here though. She was meant to catch the other situations. The ones that could risk revealing an entire secret society living right beneath the human's noses.

"Now, let's see what we've got here," she said to herself, starting the first test.

Two hours later, things weren't looking any clearer than they had been and Cassie was left frowning into a microscope, trying to work out what she was looking at but failing in a way she'd never thought possible. Even knowing what she was looking for, and with a tiny, secretive influx of magic, she hadn't got any of the answers she was looking for. On the surface, it almost seemed like shifter blood. If she was right, it was specifically avian shifter blood, but the rest of the results were making it hard for her to trust that diagnosis.

"Come on, Cassie," she muttered. "You're a smart woman, you should be able to work it out."

"They say talking to yourself is the first sign of madness."

She jumped, almost knocking over one of the vials of blood as she turned to look at the owner of the voice.

"Who are you?" She looked him up and down, trying to work it out for herself.

He certainly wasn't one of the other lab technicians, and he didn't have the air of a doctor. If she had to guess, she'd say he was paranormal too, though she'd need more time to make that assessment for sure.

"Hadrian." He held out his hand.

Not knowing what else to do, she pulled off one of her gloves and took his hand in hers, giving it a firm shake.

"What are you doing here?" She wasn't going to offer up her name for nothing. He'd somehow come into the restricted lab without anyone noticing. While the technicians kept to themselves, as a rule, they didn't let just anyone walk in and would call someone out if they weren't meant to be there.

"I've come to see you, Cassandra Morgan."

She shivered at the sound of her full name dripping from his lips. Everyone called her Cassie, and she preferred it that way. And yet there was something alluring about the way he said it that only made her want him to repeat it.

"I'm afraid I'm working. Can this wait for another time?" She struggled to tear her eyes from him as she turned away.

She knew she had to cut him off now though. He'd probably come from the Council, and if she didn't, they'd think they could get to her at any and every point during the day. And that wasn't something she was willing to have them know. Even if she worked here because of them, they still needed to respect her time and her work. She wasn't just theirs to control.

"It can't wait. It's about the sample you're working on."

The blood ran cold in Cassie's veins. How did he know what she was working on? Usually, she'd have dismissed his words as just conjecture, but with the odd behaviour of the sample she was working on, she doubted it. It just all seemed a little too suspicious for her liking.

"You have five minutes." Her voice lowered as she talked, hopefully giving him some idea of how serious it had to be for her to give up her time like that. "Give me a moment, I can take us to one of the meeting rooms."

"I don't think that's a good idea," he warned.

She closed her eyes and counted to five in her head,

trying to remain calm. She wasn't an angry person by nature, but he was pushing her last nerve.

"Fine. Come with me." She waved him in the direction of her desk.

Setting down the sample she'd been working on and her notes, she turned back to him and perched on the edge of her desk. Maybe not the most sensible position for her to be in, but she was already frustrated over the lack of answers she'd gotten and didn't have the patience for setting this up like a proper meeting.

"Speak," she demanded.

"Is it safe to here?" Hadrian raised an eyebrow.

Why did he have to be so attractive? She was sure most people wouldn't have this problem, not with the nose that looked like it had been broken one too many times and the look in his eyes that screamed cold and efficient. But to her, apparently, both of those traits were appealing. Even if they never had been before.

"There's no one about," she pointed out.

"That doesn't mean no one's listening."

"If you've come from the Council then you're well aware of what I am. Believe me when I say no one is listening." She folded her arms, partly in annoyance, but mostly so she didn't start picking things up from her desk and fidgeting with them. The last thing she wanted was to make it obvious how nervous she was.

"I'm not from the Witch Council, Miss Morgan, but I am here on important matters."

She gave him what she hoped was an expectant look.

"I believe we may have the answers you're looking for."

Cassie gave a short laugh. "Maybe I'm not looking for answers. Maybe I'm just doing my job." Despite the words, her curiosity was piqued. She wanted to know what he had to say about the blood, mostly because she hadn't made any headway on it herself.

"You're not the kind to give up when there's something to learn."

As much as she didn't want to agree, she loved finding the answers to things, and this was no different. That desire was what had made her go into science in the first place. Well, that and the urge to combine it with magic. She was sure there were some great applications of the two, and it was part of her duty to find those and prove to the Witch Council that they should be using modern science too.

"Fine. What is it you think I need to know?"

"I assume you've worked out the blood isn't human?" he asked.

"Yes. As far as I can tell, it's an avian shifter."

His eyebrows shot up faster than she can speak.

"I'm sorry, was I not supposed to have worked that out?" she asked sweetly.

"I'm just surprised you can. I wouldn't have thought any of your machines could have worked it out."

"They can't," she admitted. "It's my experience that can. There's something in their red blood cells that almost matches birds. They're quite easy to tell apart."

"Are all shifters so easy to recognise?" There was something akin to interest on his face.

She frowned. Was he seriously unaware of the various differences between different kinds of paranormal? It seemed unlikely if he knew there was something different about this specific sample she had.

"No. Sometimes you can tell it's a shifter from the sample, but it's only avian shifters I've found that are noticeblly different. You can tell witch blood just by looking at it too." She'd only been able to discover that by looking at her own blood. She'd only been half surprised to find tiny sparks of magic dancing among the blood.

"Interesting." He stroked his chin while he ran his other hand through the various papers on her desk. She wished he wouldn't do that, but it wasn't in her best interests to ask him to stop. Not when he had information that could further her own research.

"Are you going to tell me what you know about this blood?" she asked, narrowly avoiding tapping her foot with impatience.

"You're right, it's avian shifter. But it's been tampered with."

"Oh?" She turned to pick up her notebook, completely forgetting how annoyed she was by the situation as the curiosity sunk in. "Was it before or after it was extracted from the body?"

"Before," he responded.

"What was it that was introduced to the system?" She looked through her notes trying to see if there was any indication of what had happened on them.

"That's what we were hoping you could tell us."

"And you didn't think of bringing the sample to me yourself and asking me first?" She didn't try very hard to keep the accusation out of her tone. She didn't see the point in hiding something like that.

"We didn't know if you'd agree or not," Hadrian responded.

"From everything you've just told me, I think we both know that's a lie. You always knew I'd agree to look at the sample." Though she did have to hand it to him, doing it this way had meant she'd done it on the lab's time and not her own. Not that it would have made a difference to her answer. The professional intrigue would have been enough for her.

He shuffled uncomfortably from one foot to the other. "Okay, the plan was to see how far you'd get on your own. I don't think we expected you to even be able to tell what it was."

"Glad I could impress," she bit out before she could think any better of it. "Who are you here on behalf of?"

"I can't tell you that."

"Of course you can't." It was a cliché straight out of a spy movie, and she was already tired of it. She didn't want to be caught up in some weird plot she needed to get to the bottom of. And yet...

"But if you agree to help us, you might get the answers you're after."

She sighed. "Isn't that always the way?"

Hadrian's lips quirked into a smile. "I believe it is. What do you say? A little adventure in exchange for some answers?"

She pretended to think about it but knew without a doubt what her answer was going to be. "Yes."

"Welcome to the team, Cassie." He held out his hand, and she took it, giving it a firm shake and sealing the deal. Hopefully, she wasn't about to make a big mistake.

TWO

Cassie wrung her hands together, questioning what she was doing here. She should never have listened to Hadrian when he turned up at the lab. She should have sent him away and never thought about the blood sample again. Her boss might not like her failing, but that was a much less dangerous option than sitting in wait for a man she didn't know if she could trust.

Hadrian walked into the room with two other men in tow. Cassie's magic tingled in the very tips of her fingers, longing to get free. She was almost surprised she couldn't see her familiar already, this was normally a good indication that she was near. Not that she should be appearing. A witch's familiar was a private thing, and she'd only appear in front of Cassie, though legend said familiars also appeared in front of a witch's mate.

She studied each of the men in turn, wondering which one of the three had set off this reaction in her. She wasn't sure she could even discount Hadrian from that equation. There must be a reason she'd agreed to help him despite usually avoiding that kind of situation.

"Good evening, Cassandra," Hadrian greeted her.

"Please call me Cassie," she responded. It always felt so formal when she heard it.

"Good evening, Cassie, then," he corrected. "This is Issac and Zack." He indicated to each of the men as he said their name.

"Hi."

"They're the rest of my team."

"Team?" She raised an eyebrow. "I'd hardly call three people a team."

"And what would you call it?" Issac asked, a smile lifting the corners of his lips in a very endearing way. So far, it looked like he was the one most likely to be setting off her mating responses. She wouldn't mind that, he had a boyish charm about him that wasn't unattractive.

"A trio? A couple of people having a good time? Pretty much anything that's not a team."

Hadrian folded his arms and leaned against the opposite wall. "I think you'll find we are a team. Especially when it comes to paranormals, we're worth more than one person each."

She snorted. "That's the kind of elitist talk that led to the witch hunts."

"Witches, you're all the same," Zack muttered under his breath.

"Excuse me?" She rose to her feet and stared him down, daring him to explain what he meant beyond the words at the surface.

"You're all still so hung up about the witch hunts, you forget about what the rest of us have been through..."

"Still hung up about the witch hunts?" Her voice came out squeakier than she'd intended it to, but that couldn't be helped. "We're only still on about them because they never stopped. Sure, they're not sanctioned by the royal family anymore, but they're still happening. Witches disappear all the time."

"Doesn't your Council do anything about it?" Issac asked, genuine interest on his face.

"Pfft. Our Council isn't worth the chairs they sit on. Completely useless, all five of them."

Hadrian's eyebrows raised so far they almost met his hairline.

"I don't think I've heard anyone talk so badly about their Council before," Zack said darkly.

"Clearly you've never met a necromancer then," she threw back.

Issac coughed loudly. "I'm a necromancer."

"Sorry," she said instantly. "Nothing against you..."

"Oh, I know. Our Council royally screwed up with the whole trying to kill people thing. They were pretty effective with other things though." He shrugged like it wasn't a big deal, but she still regretted what she'd said. She wasn't normally so prejudiced against people, it just wound her up when other paranormals made light of what her people had been through.

"Never mind the witch hunts, for now, I'm sure we'll be assigned to deal with them later. At the moment we have a far bigger problem at hand," Hadrian interrupted, apparently having had enough of the standoff between them all.

"And that is?" She sat back down and picked up her bottle of water, taking a gulp and trying to recompose herself.

"Someone is experimenting on paranormals. That's what you saw in the blood sample at the lab."

"How did you even know about the sample?" she asked.

They exchanged looks, clearly deciding which of them should answer and what they should say.

She paid them no mind. Instead, she studied Hadrian and Zack, trying to work out what they were and which of them was setting off her mating reaction. Issac had been her first guess, but as a necromancer, she doubted he'd have that impression on her so soon. Hadrian hadn't set anything off when he'd been at the lab either, which left Zack. Which wasn't good news as far as she was concerned. Not with the huge scowl on his face and the angry looks he kept throwing in her direction. Something about her rankled him, and she didn't know what it was. Hopefully, he'd work it out before either of them had to act on the bond that was sure to grow between them.

"Well?" she prompted when she realised none of them had told her anything.

"We've suspected someone at the lab is in on the project. They'll need a scientist to head it up after all, and so we've been keeping tabs on the samples and how they've been testing. As soon as you started working on the tainted one, we knew about it," Hadrian said.

"You've been bugging the lab?" That didn't sound very secure and raised a lot more questions than it answered.

"Just the computer system," Issac put in.

"How did you even know to check our lab?" None of this was making any sense. There were hundreds of labs just like hers up and down the country. Several with other paranormals working in them too. Add in the private labs working on things like pharmaceuticals that had the right equipment, and there were probably thousands of labs they'd need to check.

"A witch with the sight told us," Issac responded. "She didn't tell us exactly when, or who would find it, but she was able to point us in the direction of the right lab."

"Yeah, the sight is like that," Cassie muttered. She hadn't been granted that particular gift, but she'd heard enough rumours to be grateful for that. The responsibilities which came with being able to see the future weren't what she wanted for herself either.

"So, here we are. Asking for your help."

"Why me?" She looked straight into Hadrian's eyes as she asked, trying not to get lost there.

"Many reasons. You're the one who was testing the blood, you're a witch, and you're a scientist. None of us have any of those things on our side, and we need someone who does."

"Circumstance then?" She wasn't sure how she felt about that. On the one hand, it was a relief to know she hadn't been set up. On the other, it kind of hurt that she wasn't unique in some other way.

"If you can call it that when there are visions of the future involved." Zack's words were almost too low to hear, so she chose to ignore them. She didn't know what his problem was, but she didn't have the patience to get to the bottom of it. At least, not yet.

"Right. So...what do you want me to do?" That was what was confusing her the most. She was just an ordinary woman with ordinary powers. She could analyse information she was given easily, but that was hardly magic. A lot of humans had that capability too.

"Work with us. We need someone to try and figure out what's been introduced into the paranormals' bloodstreams, how they might be doing it, and where they're doing it," Hadrian said.

Cassie laughed bitterly. "And you think I can tell you all that just from a blood sample? I can't even analyse it on the machines we have at the lab, never mind look for half the stuff that blood doesn't tell us either."

"That's where Zack comes in." Issac was surprisingly chirpy given the situation. "He's a pathologist."

"You're a what?" She looked at the sullen man, expecting him to at least offer some explanation.

"I think that's putting it a little too grand."

"Hardly," Issac returned. "You cut open dead bodies and try and work out what killed them. That's a pathologist in my book."

"I'm not a trained pathologist, I just have a way with bodies," he pointed out. "But you do too."

"Oh no, not me. I just have a way of talking to the dead, that's completely different," Issac countered. "Especially cause most of the time they spend more time rambling on about the state of being dead instead of how they died." For the first time since he'd arrived in the room, his sunny disposition slipped slightly.

"Will someone just tell me what's going on and what you're expecting me to do?" She was already growing frustrated with the way they were all interacting. If they kept this up, it was going to exhaust her.

"What they're trying to say is that you'll be able to work fresh from the body to do as many tests as you want," Hadrian assured her.

A thrill shot through Cassie at the thought. She'd never had an opportunity like that before, and it piqued the scientific curiosity within her.

"And you have the lab space to be able to let me do that?" She knew she was going to end up saying yes to them. But then, she'd known that the moment she'd said yes to meeting them anyway. It was too much for her to ignore the pull towards answers she'd already been seeking.

"Yes, you'll have access to a lab you'll be able to set up however you want. We have a limited budget, but it should be enough to get you the equipment you want," Hadrian acknowledged.

"Will I be allowed to infuse it with magic?" That one was important to her, and not being able to do it was one of the reasons she was struggling with the current blood sample. If she could have infused the lab equipment already, she was almost certain she would know more than she already did.

"Yes. It'll be your equipment to do whatever you want with."

"Alright. I'm in. Just tell me what you know already."

"Not much. The blood submitted to your lab was from an avian shifter, a swallow if it would interest you to know," Zack said.

"It would, thank you." She'd pulled a notepad towards her and was already scribbling notes down as he spoke.

"But he's not the first paranormal we've had in with blood irregularities. We've also had a vampire and a dryad come through with the same irregularities."

"And you're able to confirm that it's definitely the same thing introduced into the blood?" She was aware of how cold her voice had gone, but now was the time for professional curiosity and nothing more. She didn't want them to think she wouldn't do a good job.

"As far as I can tell, but I have limited experience with bloodwork so can't tell you."

"And yet you're a pathologist?" She looked up from her notes and gave him a quizzical look.

Zack gritted his teeth. "I told you, I'm not a pathologist. In some ways, I do a similar job to one, but I don't have the expertise to use the job title."

She nodded. So long as he knew his way around the body, it would do. "Whereabouts is the blood from?"

"As close to the heart as I could get. But that wasn't

very easy. There are some irregularities in the size of their hearts that can't be explained but seem to be caused by the same problem."

She nodded. That made sense from what she'd seen in the blood. "And you think the irregularities are what killed them?"

Hadrian scoffed from beside them. "Hardly. They had their throats cut."

"That'll do it," she muttered, noting it down as a cause of death. "And I assume they'd bled to death?"

"Other than the vampire, yes. But I think they'd starved her to the point where she started cannibalising her own blood."

"Not good." She'd only studied vampire blood once and had been wanting to see more ever since but knew it would be difficult to come by. There were subtle differences between theirs and human, mostly that the red blood cells looked like they had teeth. She'd love to mix the two of them together in a Petri dish and see what happened.

"No, not at all. We need to get to the bottom of this to stop anyone else falling victim."

"I can understand that." She nodded, trying to think of any other questions she might need to ask. She was worried that she was coming across too eager now that they'd started using her passion to sway her.

"If you've got time now, we can take you to our base, and you can see the information we have," Hadrian offered.

She nodded. That would definitely be more beneficial than just quizzing them here. Though she knew that once she set foot in their space, there'd be no going back. She was agreeing to help them and there wouldn't be any getting out of it.

"One last question," she said, stopping them before she got too eager.

"Yes?" Hadrian pushed away from the wall, unfolding to his full height.

"Who do you work for?" That was one of the things that bothered her the most. He'd said they didn't work for the Witch Council, but that didn't mean they didn't work for one of the others. Things were muddied by Issac though. The necromancers didn't have a Council at the moment, and it seemed unlikely he would work for any of the others.

"We work for the High Council," Issac answered.

Cassie's eyes widened. Of all the things they could have said, that wasn't what she'd expected. The High Council was shrouded in mystery. No one ever really heard from them unless they were in serious trouble. And yet there were three people who worked for them. Maybe one of them was even on it. Of course, she'd never know. The only people allowed to know the Council members' identities were the other members. It seemed like a backward situation to her. Especially when the humans were so transparent about who ran their governments.

"You okay?" Hadrian asked, leaning in and placing a comforting hand against her arm.

Sparks built around the spot he touched, springing into life in her blood and urging her to let him touch her more. It didn't make any sense. She hadn't reacted to him like this before, and yet here she was with sparks threatening to break free.

"Fine." She gave him a weak smile. "It's just a while since I've eaten. Can we stop to grab some food on the way?"

He nodded. "Of course. I should have thought about that and had some delivered."

"I can go ahead and grab some Chinese for us?" Issac suggested.

"Sounds good. Do you have anything in particular you like?" Hadrian asked her.

She shook her head. "I'm easy food-wise." And if she was going to work with the three of them, it sounded like she needed to be. Eating while working on their mystery seemed like a good way to spend their time though. The idea was certainly a fun one.

"I'll drive," Zack announced, dangling keys from one of his fingers. "Last time Hadrian drove I nearly hurled."

"Good to know," Cassie responded, still a little shaken from their revelation and the sparks in her blood.

She followed the men out to their car, hoping she'd made the right decision but doubting it with every step she took.

THREE

Empty containers cluttered the table, but she ignored them. She didn't even know where everything was in the room, so it seemed pointless trying to tidy up behind everyone.

"So, what we're saying is that there's absolutely no connection between the three victims? Not even the town they lived in or anything?" She looked down at the three sheets of paper in front of her, longing to connect the dots between them all but completely failing. The vampire looked like she was in her early twenties, but could easily have been seven or eight times that, while the dryad was in his late fifties. Not that a human would be able to tell.

"No connection at all except where the bodies were found," Hadrian said.

"Damn. And the human authorities...?"

"They picked them up at first, but we have an older vampire high up. He assigns them to us, and they get lost from the human system. If any of the boots on the ground see something they shouldn't, they get hypnotised to forget," Zack replied, picking up a leftover spring roll and crunching it down.

"That explains a lot," she said, more to herself than to them. She'd always wondered why humans didn't stumble across more paranormal related crimes, but if there was one paranormal high up keeping everyone in check, then there was likely to be more. Not that she didn't think there was a need for that. If the community wanted to stay in the shadows, then they needed to keep things under wrap.

"What it doesn't is what the connection is," Zack muttered, his moroseness never fading.

"What if we're looking too closely at it?" Cassie mused. "What if the connection isn't something to do with the people themselves, but something about their environment. Maybe they spent a lot of time alone and were easy to get hold of in order to experiment on."

"That could have some legs." Hadrian rose from his seat and strode over to the pinboard that dominated one side of the room. Up until now, Cassie had only thought those things existed in crime TV shows.

"Do you know where they were taken from?" she asked.

He shook his head. "They weren't even reported missing until a couple of days ago."

"And how long have they really been gone?" She turned to Zack, hoping he'd have an answer. While he kept saying he wasn't a proper pathologist, she believed he'd have enough experience to be able to tell her that.

"It's hard to be sure, but I reckon they've been in captivity but alive for between one month and two. There are different levels of decay in their bodies too. Some is from when their bodies were dumped, but I'm sure some are from mistreatment. Particularly in the vampire's case."

A short hiss came from Hadrian's direction, but she ignored it. Between the dark hip flask he'd revealed from his jacket pocket, and the lack of shifter vibes coming from him, she'd already worked out he was a vampire, and mistreatment of his kind was going to sting.

"Have the Councils been made aware?" she asked, looking between the three of them.

"The Vampire Elders aren't interested. They have other things to occupy them," Hadrian muttered.

"What could be more important than people dying?" She frowned, trying to work out what it could be. Surely nothing as scandalous as the Necromancer Council falling apart.

Hadrian sighed. "One of the Elders assaulted another one's mate. They're pretty much at war with one another trying to get the rest of them to back them. It's a complete mess."

"It sounds it." And meant they wouldn't get any help from them either. "What about the dryads and the shifters?"

"Both have been informed. They have an alliance, so they'll be working closely with us when we need their juris-diction," he confirmed.

"And the High Council wouldn't be doing that anyway?" She had to wonder what the point was of working for the High Council if they didn't do anything more than tell people what they needed to do.

"The High Council doesn't do things so much as give instructions," Zach pointed out. "And not always instruc-tions people want to get."

She grimaced, not liking to think that was how the people at the top of the political chain ran things.

"Okay." She turned back to the papers, not sure what she was looking for but hoping something jumped out at her. Either a break in the case already, or the reason why they'd picked her.

She was far from the only paranormal working in a lab. She'd even heard about another witch working in one of the pharmaceutical labs not far away. They could easily have gone for her, she'd have just as much expertise. Maybe not specifically in blood but she'd have the intelligence to pick it up quickly enough.

"And discovering the bodies was only a recent thing?" she asked.

Issac nodded. "The first one showed up about a week ago."

"So, not long at all." She got up and started to pace, trying to work out what to make of all the information she'd been given. There had to be some way for them to make sense of this.

"Long enough for three people to meet their maker." Zack's gaze cut into her, and she regretted her poor word choice.

"I doubt it's only three," she responded. "If they're testing, then there'll at least be a fourth person they're working on now."

"At least?" Hadrian pushed himself away from the wall and sat down on the chair she'd left vacant.

As far as she could tell from the layout of the room, they hadn't expected to bring a fourth person into the team. Everything was set up in threes, including the seats at the table.

"It makes no sense for them to get rid of their test subjects unless they have a replacement. If I'm honest, I'm surprised they've dumped the bodies at all."

"What do you mean?" Issac leaned forward, his attention on her every word.

"Just that if they're trying to do some kind of experiment, then a dead body could tell them just as much as a live one. Potentially more in some situations," Cassie explained as she walked back and forth.

"That's true," Zack added, surprising her. She hadn't thought he'd ever side with her, especially not so early on in them knowing one another. He was the kind of man that needed some time to soften up, and she didn't think that was anything to do with her being a woman either. It had everything to do with him as a person.

"Which brings us back to why they've dumped the bodies. Other than the hearts, was there anything wrong with them?" She wasn't sure what she'd do with his answer, she didn't know enough about anatomy for that. Her only hope was that he said something that connected the few dots she held so far.

"No, nothing. Just the heart and the blood," Zack responded.

"Are we sure the blood isn't toxic?"

"Maybe if it was ingested, but I've had my hands all over those bodies and it hasn't shown any signs of destroying any of the protective clothing I've been wearing."

"Could it be infected with a contagious disease?" While most paranormals were immune to illness other than under extreme circumstances, she couldn't help thinking of the human blood disorders that could be transferred between people.

"I suppose it could, are there tests you could do to look for one?" Hadrian asked.

"None that exist, but I'm sure I could create one if I set my mind to it." In fact, that was precisely the kind of challenge she enjoyed.

"Good, hopefully, that will get us closer to the answers

we..." Hadrian was cut off by the shrill ring of the telephone.

Each of the men exchanged glances like they knew what was coming. In a way, Cassie reckoned she knew too. It wasn't hard to guess given their reactions.

Hadrian didn't waste any time and strode over to the desk phone, picking it up and mumbling into it.

"I hope you have a coat with you." Zack's eyes had turned cold.

"Yes, why?"

"Where we're about to go, it's going to be chilly."

The corners of her lips curled up into a smile. "I'm a witch, even if I didn't have a coat, I have my ways of staying warm." She didn't add how nice it was that she could admit she was a witch out loud. Working with humans, it was something she kept quiet in fear of accidentally letting the existence of the paranormal world slip. No one had actually been punished for it in her memory, but some of the communities were a lot more secretive than others, and she imagined some of them just kept it quiet when they had someone to punish.

"We have another body," Hadrian announced as he set the phone down.

"Are we going now?" Issac asked, already grabbing his coat from the rack.

"Yes, they're holding it at the crime scene now. Seems our vampire contact was on the scene quickly enough to hand it over without any of the human police getting involved."

"We'll be needing a forensic kit, then," Zack said, leaving the room without doing anything else. She presumed he was off to get the equipment he needed but had no way of knowing for sure.

"Can we do forensics?" she asked the other two.

"To an extent. We can get samples for you and Zack, but DNA itself is pretty much useless when it comes to us. None of the Councils use a system like the humans do, which means we can't check off names against it," Hadrian responded.

"How annoying."

Issac chuckled. "It is rather. Our job would be a lot easier if we could."

"We just have to rely on a lot more old-fashioned detective work." Hadrian shrugged as if it was no big deal, but she could see in his eyes that he was kind of annoyed by the fact. She had to admit, it would annoy her too in his situation. If the paranormal communities got better at keeping track of everyone, there'd be far fewer problems than there were now.

"Is there no chance there are humans involved in this?"

Zack gave a short laugh as he reentered the room with a huge black case in his left hand. "Humans don't have the power to do this to paranormals."

Cassie whirled around, sparks threatening at her fingertips. The angriness inside her wanted to launch a barrage at him. "Tell that to the thousands of witches who have lost their lives to the witch hunts over the years." She stepped forward, letting the red sparks dance around her hand, knowing it created a slightly sinister glow around her from the times she'd tested it in the mirror. "Have you ever been to the Witch Council building? Have you seen the list? It covers entire walls with the names of the men, women, and children who lost their lives. And do you know the worst bit?"

Zack shook his head.

"The last time that list was added to was three weeks ago. Not centuries like everyone believes, not even years. But weeks. So don't tell me that humans can't hurt paranormals. Because they do and this could very well be linked back to them."

Issac's hand rested on her shoulder, though she wasn't entirely sure how she was so sure it was him and not Hadrian behind her. "We've tested the DNA and we haven't found anything that didn't belong to the victims, but that doesn't mean there isn't anything else. We'll definitely keep an open mind about the human angle."

His words had a surprisingly calming effect on her. She'd have gone as far as to say he was using some kind of magic on her except that she knew necromancers needed to hum or sing for that and he was doing nothing.

"Thank you," she whispered, letting the magic fade from her hands.

She turned to Issac and gave him a weak smile, not missing the angry look Hadrian threw at Zack over her shoulder. Maybe he realised she could still walk away from whatever she was getting into. She didn't know anything particularly sensitive yet. Clearly, they needed her more than she'd realised.

"We need to get going, Richard won't be able to hold the human police off forever. If we're not there in the next half an hour, they'll move in," he announced.

"We'd better get going then," Cassie responded, pulling herself together and trying to ignore the slight anger still bubbling away in her. As annoyed as she was with Zack's assumptions about the witch hunts, she knew she should direct that into finding out who was behind the deaths. Paranormal or human, the guilty party was bad news for everyone.

FOUR

The natural light was almost gone as they approached the stark white tent that had been put up around the body, replaced by artificial lights within it. As much as Cassie knew it was uncouth, she couldn't help the slight excitement welling up within her. She'd never been to a crime scene before, but a small part of her had always been curious to see one. And now she was finally going to get the chance.

"What are we looking at?" Hadrian asked a tall man standing outside.

"Same as your last one," the man replied, at which point Cassie realised this must be the vampire contact he'd talked about.

"How long have they been gone?" Issac asked, hurrying to Hadrian's side.

"Not long enough that you can't do your magic."

She watched as the necromancer's shoulders sagged in relief and wondered what it could possibly mean. It didn't make any sense that he was relieved about a fresh body.

"You're about to see something very few people ever have," Zack whispered to her.

"Cryptic," Cassie muttered, wondering if they were ever going to be more forthcoming about things.

Zack held open the flap of the tent, letting her duck through first and surprising her completely. He hadn't seemed like the kind of man who would suddenly change his tune, and this was out of character. Unless it wasn't and he was just trying to protect himself by being a bit more prickly.

"They've already bagged most of the evidence and taken swabs," Hadrian told the two of them. "Thankfully, we still have it all." He indicated towards a couple of black cases stacked against the wall.

"Good. We can work on those back at the lab," Zack responded.

She couldn't help but feel a little disappointed. She'd hoped she'd get to see an actual crime scene in action, but it looked like most of the big stuff had been done.

"Suit up, then we'll get the other units gone, and Issac can do his bit."

Zack nodded and took Cassie's arm, bringing her off to the side. He dug through his case and pulled out a sealed plastic bag with something white in it. Excitement bubbled inside her at the thought of putting on one of the infamous white suits. Until she remembered she was here because someone was dead and she shouldn't be looking at it as something to get excited about.

"Thanks." She took the bag, ripping it open and getting into the white jumpsuit. The crunchiness of the plastic was almost surprising, but she ignored it. There was too much going on to let herself get distracted.

The man Hadrian had talked to left the tent, though she could hear the faint rumbling of his voice as he spoke to the human police force outside, probably dismissing them so they could do their own thing.

"Alright, you ready, Issac?" Hadrian asked.

The necromancer nodded and stepped towards the body. "What do we know about her?"

"Not much. Her name is Tyann and she's a lion shifter," Hadrian read from a notebook.

Cassie sucked in a breath, three sets of eyes turning to her at the sound.

"Is everything okay?" Zack asked. He'd moved automatically, his hand hovering over the small of her back, not quite touching but hanging there almost like he wanted to.

She ignored the sensation. Now wasn't the time for getting into the complexities of the bond forming with Zack. She didn't even know what kind of paranormal he was yet.

"I know her," Cassie whispered. Deep within, she knew any doubts of her not helping the men were gone entirely now. She might not have known Tyann well, but it was enough to make this more personal than it had been before.

"How?" Issac asked.

"She went to my yoga class. She wasn't at the last three or four, I can't remember. We thought she must have moved cities." Cassie gave the body a sad glance really taking her in for the first time and trying not to see the red slash across her throat. It was hard to see the formerly upbeat shifter in this position.

"Is it best if Cassie does the talking, then?" Issac asked Hadrian.

He shook his head. "You still know what questions to ask, but we'll keep her close in case we need her to step in."

Issac nodded. He'd lost some of his jovial air now they

were in the tent and close to the body, but that made sense to her. She didn't know anyone who wouldn't be affected by the situation. And would judge people if they could be happy around a body.

"Let's get going then." Issac pulled a ceremonial looking knife from his pocket and rolled up on of his sleeves, making a deep slash there.

Cassie couldn't take her eyes from the red rivulet of blood flowing down his pale skin. There was something beautiful about it, and yet something deadly. Issac didn't have the same fascination and began to hum a slow, sad tune. Purple smoke rose from the cut on his arm and he batted it around with his hand before sending it in the direction of Tyann's mouth.

Necromancer magic wasn't something she'd ever seen performed. In fact, it was something very few people ever saw performed. They were secretive at the best of times. She'd never even dreamed of being able to see it.

The body began to twitch as the magic slipped in through parted lips. Cassie wanted to ask what was going on but knew it was better not to interrupt the attention of someone doing magic. This was clearly a well thought out part of what the men did.

She almost jumped out of her skin as Tyann's body sat bolt upright and let out a chilling scream.

Zack's hand finally made it all the way to the small of her back. "It's okay, that's supposed to happen," he whispered.

She nodded, grateful for his reassurance even if she wasn't too sure where it was coming from.

"Tyann?" Issac asked.

She turned to him sharply, staring at him with dead eyes. This was nothing like Cassie had expected when she'd thought about raising the dead before, and it just led to more questions than ever.

"Where am I?" the lioness asked, her voice echoing around the tent and sounding like nothing short of death.

"I'm so sorry, Tyann, you died," Issac said softly.

"I died?"

"Yes. And we're trying to find your killer. But we don't have much to go on, and we hoped you'd be able to tell us something about what happened." It was clear that Issac's tone was aiding the dead woman in not freaking out. Cassie wouldn't have blamed her if she had. There must have been something terrifying about what had happened to her.

"I don't remember."

"You have to try, please," Issac responded.

The dead woman didn't say a word.

"Tyann?" Cassie's voice shook as she said the woman's name and the dead eyes turned to her, piercing within and seeing into her soul.

"I know you."

"Yes. We did yoga together. I'm sorry about what happened to you."

Issac started to say something but Hadrian held up his hand, effectively silencing him.

"Me too."

"Were there other people imprisoned with you?" she asked.

"Yes. Three. At least, three that I met. From the screams, I think there might have been more." The lioness shivered as she recalled what was going on.

"Do you know where you were?"

Tyann shook her head, the whites of her eyes never moving and only adding to the odd atmosphere within the tent. "I'm sorry. I don't think I was killed here."

"You're right, there isn't enough blood," Hadrian answered.

"I was taken while I was asleep. I didn't even scream." She looked down at her hands, still stuck in the claws of death. Apparently, Issac's magic only worked on parts of her body.

"Tyann, we don't have much time left with you, is there anything else you can tell us about what happened?" Issac asked.

"Nothing that will help. They did things to us. They were always testing what we could do, but they never told us what it was for. Apparently, only the villains in TV shows do that."

Zack snorted.

"Did you recognise any of them? Or even what they were?" Cassie asked, hoping they could at least know if they were looking for paranormal or human culprits.

"I'm sorry, no. They wore masks. There were so many smells around I couldn't work what they were."

"That's okay," Cassie whispered.

Issac tapped his wrist. Cassie nodded. Tyann didn't have long left in this state now.

"We need you to lie back down now, Tyann." Cassie stepped forward and crouched down, putting her hand over the other woman's, hoping she'd be able to feel the comfort she was offering. "I promise you, we're going to find out who did this. We'll make sure your death isn't in vain."

"Thank you." Tyann's eyelids fluttered closed, covering the eerie white eyes.

No one needed to tell Cassie she'd slipped away once more. Or that there was nothing else that could be done to save her. At least the information the lioness had given them could be used to make sure they didn't waste any time. Not that it put them any further ahead than they had been before.

Cassie sat back on her heels, not quite knowing what to do next. A solemn air had settled in the tent, each of the team lost in their own thoughts. She understood that. There was so much confusion surrounding a death. Even more so when they'd talked to her.

"Is that what all the necromancy fuss is about?" she asked eventually.

Issac stopped what he was doing and threw her a weak smile. "No. That was just communicating with the dead, not raising them."

Her eyebrow shot up. "So you can do more than that?"

He shrugged. "Theoretically. I've never tried it."

"Is that normal? For a necromancer I mean."

"Yes. There's a surprising number of us who don't do that. It's not a great experience."

"I thought you hadn't done it?" She finally rose to her feet and busied herself with tidying some of the area around her, only focusing on things she knew she wouldn't mess up for the team. If they'd had longer to prep, she might have been more useful, but she tried not to focus on what could have been.

"I haven't, but I have witnessed it," he replied. "Necromancer learning is a little unusual."

She snorted. "Just a little?"

"Point taken. But I saw it when I was seven and vowed on that day I'd never do it. It took Hadrian a lot of persuading to even get me to go this far." He gestured sadly to Tyann's rapidly cooling body.

"He was a tough nut to crack," Hadrian said from above. "But I knew I'd get him eventually. He's too good of a man to let crimes go unsolved."

"So that's your main move then? Find people you think

will help because of who they are?" She already knew he was going to say yes, but something within her made her ask anyway.

"In a fashion. I choose people I have a good feeling about. I'm never wrong."

"And your good feeling has only extended to three people other than yourself?" Surprise seeped into her voice.

"I haven't looked very hard. I find small teams work best together."

Cassie didn't respond, she couldn't find the words to. If he liked to keep things small and intimate, what had made him come after her? She wasn't anything special, which she was sure he knew. There must have been another reason he picked her. Ignoring the obvious idea that he was the one setting off her mating response and that was why he wanted her. She refused to accept that was true. She was worth more than just being someone's mate.

"I'm done," Zack announced. "I can't do anything else until we're back at the lab."

"Alright then, pack up, we'll take Tyann back now and drop Cassie back home on the way," Hadrian announced.

"I can get a cab," she suggested.

Zack laughed. "I don't think you'll be doing much cab-taking any more."

She didn't ask what that meant. She didn't need to. It seemed like the three of them had adopted her into their team and there was no going back to how things had been without them. Deep down, she kind of liked that. Other than the dead bodies, though even they held their fascination.

FIVE

The same face as always looked back into the mirror at her. Just one change needed to be made. She ran her hands through her hair, turning it from turquoise to a vibrant purple with only a handful of sparks. It was one of the things she enjoyed the most about the ability to do magic. It wasn't all work and no play.

"This is Donna speaking, how can I help?" the receptionist chirped down the phone.

"Hi, Donna, it's Cassie Morgan. I'm so sorry, but I'm not feeling great." She did a fake cough, hoping it wouldn't spark any suspicion in the other woman. Though she doubted it. Donna had never seemed like the smartest of women, though Cassie suspected some of it was an act.

"Oh no, honey, you don't sound great."

Cassie winced. She hated lying but knew she didn't have any choice if she wanted to help the team with their investigation. Only some of her lying was to do with the promise of the lab they said she could use. "I don't think I'm going to be able to make it in..."

"That's okay, I'll let Michael know."

"Thanks, Donna. So sorry. I'll let you know how I'm feeling tomorrow."

"Just rest up and drink plenty of hot tea," the woman instructed.

She just about held back from rolling her eyes. Why was it that no matter who she told she was ill, they gave her instructions on how to take care of herself? Not only was she a fully-grown woman, but she was a scientist. She was well aware of what to do to make her feel better.

"Thanks. Hopefully, I'll see you tomorrow." She felt guilty for calling in sick, but it wasn't something she'd ever done before. She didn't need to. Most paranormals weren't susceptible to illness in the same way humans were. She'd been called in to cover other people being ill a lot too, so she was happy she'd paid her dues.

Hitting the red button to end the call, she turned away from her dresser and towards the overflowing wardrobe, wondering what the standard outfit for investigating a murder was. Jeans and a comfy shirt seemed like the best option, if a little bit informal. But that was all the guys had been wearing the day before.

Settling on her choice, she dressed quickly and made her way out of her flat. Hadrian had already text to say he'd meet her outside and she didn't want to keep him waiting. She knew as well as anyone that every minute could count if they wanted to catch whoever was behind Tyann's murder before another body showed up.

"I wondered how quickly you'd make your way downstairs," he said the moment she exited her building.

"I didn't want to hold up anything important."

He took a sip from his coffee cup before offering her the one in his other hand. "I didn't know what you wanted but then remembered you were a witch, if you don't like it, you can change it. Right?"

Her eyes crinkled as she smiled. "Yes, I can change it. But what is it?"

"Tea, no sugar."

"Then it's perfect already." She reached out to take the cup, their fingers brushing against each other and sparks formed in her hands. She tried to call them back, but they had a mind of their own and jumped along Hadrian's skin as well as her own.

"Ah. I wondered when that would happen," he observed.

"You knew?"

He shook his head and pushed away from the wall, starting to walk down the street at a leisurely pace. "I suspected. I've wanted to bite you since the moment we met and not in the food way. That's generally a good indication for vampires."

"I imagine it is. But I don't get it, you didn't set me off when we met at my lab."

"I think that's because you hadn't met Zack and Issac yet."

She snorted. "I don't know how mating works for vampires, but it doesn't work like that for us witches. We just meet our mate and then we're done," she countered.

"Maybe you don't just have one mate."

"Highly improbable. I've looked into the multiple mate thing, and it doesn't happen as often as people seem to think. It's just because each one is a minor scandal that other people talk about it all the time."

"Highly improbable doesn't mean it's not you."

"True. But if all three of you were my mates, then surely I would have a better indication of it? I should be sparking all over the place." She kept the various sparking urges she'd had over the past few days quiet. She didn't want to accept they were happening, or what they might mean for her going forward.

"Deny it all you want, but I think you'll find yourself in for a rocky ride. I don't need to tell you what happens to paranormals who deny their mates."

She shuddered. No, he did not. The consequences ranged from murdering sprees to going insane. None of which she found particularly appealing. "I'll think about it."

"Good. None of us are going anywhere, I haven't talked to the other two yet either, but I suspect they already know who you are to them."

"Is that why Zack is being so prickly?" She didn't mean to ask, but the question just slipped out without any thought.

"He's just like that." Hadrian shrugged. "I've known him for a long time, and even I don't know what caused it. He just doesn't seem to like people very much."

"It'd almost be better if he were the vampire," she quipped.

"Close. He's a bat shifter, actually."

Her mouth fell open and then snapped shut as she considered the implications of that. Unless Hadrian was pulling her leg, his theory that all three of them were her mates was looking a little more robust. Her familiar had been a bat made of sparks her entire life, and she'd heard enough rumours about witch and shifter matings to know what was the cause of her familiar's form.

"I like the hair," he said after a few more steps.

"Thanks. I like changing it up."

"It suits you."

"You have to say that, you're my..." She snapped her mouth shut, holding back the final word before she committed to it. She wasn't ready for that, and he knew that as well as she did.

Hadrian chuckled. "I don't have to say anything. I really like it."

"Are we going by car?" She frowned, trying to work out where he could have parked. There was plenty of space outside her building, and yet they were still walking down the street.

"It's a nice day, I thought we'd walk to the lab and give ourselves a bit of time to talk."

"Isn't it too far?"

"It only seemed that way last night because you didn't know where you were going," he responded, and she had to accept that there was a truth in that. Last night had all been about the wonder in the moment.

"It's good to know it's close to home," she responded. One of the only things she disliked about her current job was the commute. It always took so long to get there by public transport but having a car would be an unnecessary expense. It was only then she realised she was already thinking about working on the case as a job and replaced her own with it. Which was a little premature, especially as she didn't know if they'd even keep her around after they'd solved the murders. Or if she'd get paid, though if the three mates thing was real then maybe she didn't even need to earn a wage, she could just live off what they earned.

She almost scoffed at the thought, not wanting to be the kind of woman that needed a man to live her life.

"We're just around the corner now, we'll be there in a second."

"It's a lovely walk," she observed.

"It is. We live in a beautiful city."

"Mmm," she agreed, though secretly she thought it was

much the same as any other city in the country. She was more of a country girl at heart and had only moved there because it was the only place she could get the job she wanted but explaining that seemed too complicated at this point in time.

"Did you discover anything overnight?" she asked instead.

"No, we haven't been to the lab yet. You'll learn everything we do, as we learn it."

She perked up at that. The last thing she'd expected was to be as involved as that. She wouldn't have blamed them if they wanted to keep her in the dark. They barely knew her even if they were all mates.

"Don't they call you if there's something big?" she asked.

"At this stage, only if there's a body. And only if Richard is about to divert it to us. He has enough going on that he's not always in."

"Who is he? Other than another vampire." She'd been dying to ask, but there'd been more important things going on at the time.

Hadrian chuckled. "You got that much from him?"

She nodded but didn't say anything else.

"We don't really know. I assume he's employed by the High Council like we are. Though I do think Zack has a feeling he's one of the members. We have no way of knowing for sure though."

"You've never met the High Council?" She pushed down the disappointment welling up within her. A small part of her had hoped they'd shed some light on the mysterious higher power.

"Not many people get to," he pointed out.

"I knew that. I just thought..."

"Cassie, there are paranormals up and down the

country who work for the Council but have never met them. Have you met your own?"

She shook her head. "But I know where to find them if I need them," she responded.

"And I know how to get in contact with the High Council. As do each of the individual Councils. That's how it works. We're at the bottom of the food chain and they're at the top." He shrugged as if that was the end of it.

"Except that you're not, are you?" she countered. "You're at least part of the way up the food chain."

He sighed. "I guess at a push, yes, I am. But that's the way it's always been. In the past we may have called them kings and queens, but it's exactly the same concept. They're untouchable to most, accessible to some, and controllable by none."

"I hadn't looked at it that way," she admitted. Really, she tried not to think about the Councils much at all. It just reminded her of how close to the bottom she really was.

"We're here," he announced, pushing open a door for her.

"That wasn't far at all." She stepped through, smirking at him in thanks.

"No, definitely an easy commute."

She didn't respond, she was too busy fixating on the word commute and what it might mean for her future. Clearly, this wasn't just a temporary position to the men. Not that she was going to ask about it today, they needed to get used to her first. Especially Zack.

"Where am I heading first?" she asked instead.

"Zack wants to start investigating the body as soon as he can. Do you know how to scrub up?" He stepped into the brightly-lit hall, letting the door to the outside world swing closed behind him.

She nodded. It was one of the things she'd learned how to do at the lab in case there was an emergency where she had to go into a sterile environment. The likelihood had always been slim, but it was better safe than sorry. At least, that had been the company's official line. Whether they believed it or not was another thing.

"Perfect, just head straight down and take a left at the end. Once you're scrubbed in, Zack will take you through the rest."

"Thank you." She turned away from him.

"Cassie?"

She spun back around at the need in his voice. Something about it called to her and made her need to respond. "Yes?"

"Have a good day. I'll see you in a bit?" She couldn't ignore the hope burning in his eyes as he asked.

"Yes, I'll see you in a bit," she responded, knowing she'd do everything she could to make that true.

But first, she had a dead body to go see.

SIX

"I was wondering when you'd get here," Zack said, not looking up from the laptop he was using.

"It's eight am," she pointed out. Even by early bird standards, it wasn't late. She needed to remember what Hadrian had said about him being a bat shifter, maybe that had something to do with his confusion over the time.

"Hmm."

"What do you want me to do?" she asked, looking around the lab and trying to work out where to start. A lump caught in her throat as her eyes rested on the still form covered by a white sheet.

Tyann.

Her heart went out to the lioness. It couldn't have been easy for her to be as imprisoned as she was.

"Do you want to take notes while I do the autopsy?" he asked, surprisingly kindly given his usual briskness. Maybe Zack was coming around to her after all. Or perhaps it was simpler than that. They were in his domain after all.

"Okay." Cassie had no idea if she even had the stomach for what was about to happen. She'd always wanted to see a real-life autopsy, but ultimately, there was a reason she'd become a lab technician and not a doctor of some kind.

"Normally I record myself, I'm going to do that too, if that's okay?"

"Of course, whatever you need to do." The last thing she wanted was to be getting in the way of his job. Not when it could help them solve the case.

"Thank you. I might need you to consult the laptop too at times."

"Why?" She frowned, unable to think what might be so important that he needed to check it in the middle of an autopsy?

"With humans, it's straightforward to judge when they died, how long they've been malnourished for, things like that. With paranormals, it's a bit more difficult. We're all built differently and have different levels of some chemicals. So, I might need you to check what the charts say about shifters before I make assumptions."

She nodded. "That makes sense." She glanced at the laptop, still a little confused about how he was getting all the information. "Have you dealt with enough bodies to make the charts yourself?"

Zack gave a dry chuckle. "I wish. But no, there's about a dozen paranormal pathologists in the world, and we all talk to one another to get the information."

"Ah." There was something nice about the idea of them all working together to collate information. It certainly went quite a way to soften Zack in her eyes.

"Right, let's get on with it." Despite his harsh words, Zack approached Tyann's body reverently, pulling the sheet back slowly.

They spent the next couple of hours working surprisingly well with one another. Zack clearly enjoyed talking to himself as he worked, but Cassie found that it helped her take the notes he wanted, especially as he went into so much detail on each part.

"Do you need any more samples?" he asked her, not looking up from Tyann's liver.

"The more I have, the more I can test, but I don't need anything specific," she replied. Blood might be her speciality, but she'd worked in other parts of the lab when covering other people and was reasonably confident she'd be able to test some of the tissue samples they'd collected too. Not that it mattered if she couldn't. It wasn't like they could send the sample out to an actual lab, it would be far too risky with all the non-paranormals about. Not to mention pointless. She doubted Hadrian would have brought her on board in the first place if it was as simple as that.

"Great, we just need to put Tyann back, then we'll go to our meeting. Let's hope Hadrian and Issac have found more than we have." He snapped off his stained rubber gloves and threw them away. Rolling on a new pair, he grabbed the sheet from where it rested before covering Tyann back up and sliding her back into storage.

The metal door clanged shut, sealing the dead lioness inside and sending shivers down Cassie's spine. If she wasn't careful, she was going to end up having nightmares about being trapped inside one of the awful freezer lockers.

"Right, let's go."

"Don't we need to write a report?" she stuttered. It was what all the pathologists did in the TV shows she liked to watch, though she knew not all of what happened in them was factually correct.

"I have one." He tapped his head and turned away.

"Your head is your report?" She couldn't help the note

of scorn that slipped into her voice. It wasn't very professional of him to act that way.

"It's as good as we need. At the moment, we have nothing more to go on than what I've seen anyway. You haven't had time to do any tests."

"That's not my fault," she bit out. She wasn't sure why she was rising to him so much, she knew better than to act this way, and yet, Zack seemed to be bringing out the worst in her.

He sighed. "I'm sorry, you're right it isn't. But Hadrian always wants a meeting after the autopsy."

She nodded. "Okay, I guess let's go?"

The two of them just stood there, neither giving ground. She wasn't even sure what they were doing by standing off against one another at all. They had nothing to gain from it.

"Where is the meeting?" she asked eventually, feeling slightly uncomfortable with the charged air around them. He was having an effect on her whether she liked it or not, and her sparks were close to the surface again, ready to fill the air with their bright red magic.

"I'll show you." He turned around without so much as another glance, making her feel surprisingly abandoned. She squashed the feeling. If what Hadrian had said was correct, then this was nothing more than Zack acting out because he could.

SEVEN

"**S**o, here's what we know," Hadrian said again.

Cassie just about refrained from rolling her eyes. It wasn't that she found the process itself boring, more than she knew they weren't actually going to get anywhere, no matter how much they tried to. Not with the little they had to go on.

"We have four victims who don't have anything connecting them at all, not even paranormal type. Each lives within a hundred miles of here..."

"But that tells us nothing," Issac interrupted. "There was that serial killer whose victims were all hours from home, he just used the motorways to get to them."

"And it tells us even less if the culprit is a paranormal," Cassie added. "We have our own ways of travelling without being detected."

"Precisely. And of removing any biological evidence. Was there any sign of a struggle?" Hadrian turned to Zack as he asked.

The shifter leaned back in his seat, looking even more fed up with the situation than Cassie was. Potentially because he knew they'd have more answers if the two of them were allowed to head back down to the lab and do more tests.

He shrugged. "It's hard to tell in the shape the bodies are in. All of them have superficial wounds to them. If I had to guess, I'd say they were from some kind of torture. Potentially to get them to do what their captors wanted rather than fighting them at every turn. But that's just conjecture."

"But there weren't any signs of fighting with Tyann?" Hadrian asked.

Zack shook his head. "It's like she said, she didn't fight. No recent marks on her. The only thing I did notice this time was that she had some skin flakes under her finger-nails but we don't know how old they are."

"The others didn't have that?" Issac asked.

"I don't know. I actually didn't look. It was only because of Cassie's comment about a potential human link that I did. DNA wouldn't help us if it was another para-normal doing this." Zack looked at her, then glanced away quickly, almost as if he didn't want to admit he'd taken her suggestion seriously.

"Do we still have the bodies?"

"Yes, but the degradation might make it difficult to find anything," Zack admitted.

"How about if I find something, we can test the other ones?" Cassie suggested.

"That makes sense." Zack nodded. "It's a waste of our time and expense if we don't get a positive result from Tyann's samples."

Cassie relaxed into her chair, silently pleased he was at least respecting her opinion in terms of intelligence, even if he didn't seem to like her much in any other way.

"Alright. When will you know?" Hadrian asked her.

"There are a few basic checks I can do today on it to discern whether it's human or paranormal DNA. Anything other than that will take a lot longer, but at least it will give us a direction we can work in."

"Yes, definitely. That's better than nothing." Hadrian turned to Issac. "I take it there's no movement on if there are any witnesses?"

"No. No one's seen anything. Tyann lived alone, just like the others, and didn't have any appointments or meetings in the days she disappeared. It was her employer that reported her, but it was only after she hadn't turned up to work for a full week."

"Which doesn't really narrow it down. She could have been taken at any point between Friday night and Monday morning and we'd be none the wiser." Hadrian sighed.

"What about looking into places that could be the location of the facility Tyann mentioned?" Cassie suggested, suppressing the nerves about speaking up. "There can't be that many around. Especially not if they don't want people to hear the screaming." She cringed as she said the word, but knew it was better to accept it for what it was rather than avoiding the situation. Mistakes would be made if they didn't work under the true premise.

"There could be something in that, but I think we need to widen the search parameters to find it," Issac mused. "Just looking around here seems to be a mistake. We haven't found anything that points in the right direction yet, and I think there's a good reason for that."

Hadrian nodded. "Alright, but if you want to do that, then we need to ask about in the network as well. There's only three of us, and we just don't have the manpower to spend on a cross-country search."

"I'll send out the alert as soon as we're done here."

Issac scribbled something on his notepad, presumably to remind himself to do what he'd promised.

"No one else has found any bodies, have they?" Hadrian asked Zack.

"Not that have been reported, though there's always a chance they've slipped through the net and haven't been discovered by us yet."

"Is that not dangerous?" she asked, already worrying about what human pathologists might find if they examined a paranormal body.

"Not as dangerous as you think. We have alerts in place for anybody or DNA that proves problematic, and most of the labs working with the morgues have at least one employee of the High Council working there to ensure that anything that needs to be swept under the table is," Zack replied.

"But when the person is dead...?" She just couldn't make sense of it. Surely there would be things that just didn't make any sense to humans.

"I suspect a lot of the pathologists working with the police do suspect there's more that exists than just them. But they'd be called crazy if they turned around to the detectives and told them that their murder victim was actually a vampire and it might have been a wolf shifter who'd killed them," Hadrian explained.

"Fair point." It still seemed risky, but then there'd always been theories about the supernatural elements of the world. Some had even come close to the truth, and yet the paranormal communities hadn't even come close to discovery since the witch hunts, and even they had killed more humans than they had paranormals.

"So far, nothing has pinged any of my alerts, but I can do a manual search while Cassie tests the blood and other fluids we took from the body."

"Thank you. The more we're certain of, the better," Hadrian replied. "So far, there doesn't seem to be a pattern in when the victims are showing up either."

"Maybe that's because it's not actually supposed to be a pattern." Cassie pushed her chair back, scraping it along the floor. She winced at the sound but pushed past it.

The information boards in front of her were overflowing with notes, though she suspected that most of them were half-baked theories and notes on what to pursue next. But among the post-it notes and scribbled reminders, the crucial bits of the case were written.

"The dumping ground is the same every time," she mused. "Why?"

"I assume they think no one will find the bodies there," Issac responded, watching her with keen interest.

"How long after death did you find the bodies?"

"We're not sure about the vampire, it was hard to tell when she died. But three days for the avian shifter, he was the first. One day for the dryad, and a couple of hours for Tyann," Zack read from his notes.

"So, the first one was there for a while? Who found the body?" She didn't look at them as she asked, trying to find the information she needed on the boards but failing miserably.

"One second, I'll check the police report." Hadrian strode over to a set of metal drawers and pulled it open, rifling through for whatever report it was that he needed. "The police said it was an anonymous tip-off. They never talked to the person that dumped the body after the initial call, but it was a well-spoken man. The operator suggested he was in his thirties, though it's hard to tell over the phone and there's a lot of room for error."

"Barely helpful at all," Zack muttered.

"How long after the body was found was it handed over to you?" she asked.

"A couple of weeks. We have all the information the police gathered, but it doesn't tell us very much. Their autopsy found nothing and destroyed most of the evidence Zack could have found..."

"Wait, the human pathologist did an autopsy?" She spun around, looking straight at Zack.

"Yes. Made a right mess of it too. Why?" He narrowed his eyes, probably trying to work out if she was blaming him for something she shouldn't be.

"If the human pathologist did his job, there should have been a swab from under the avian shifter's fingernails." She looked pointedly at Hadrian, hoping he'd find the information she hoped he would.

"Ah, yes, here it is." He withdrew what looked like an autopsy report and held it out to her.

Cassie shook her head. "Zack will be able to make more sense of it than I can."

"Ah." Hadrian placed it on the table and slid it over to the bat shifter who took it instantly and started reading intently.

Her heart pounded in her chest. She hoped her hunch was right. If they had the sample still on file, she'd be able to compare it to the one they had now, and at least they'd know it was the same person they were looking for.

"We have it!" Zack sounded more excited than she'd even thought possible from him. "We have the sample in the lab downstairs. It was never sent off for testing because they didn't have a suspect to match it against."

"That seems like an oversight." Cassie's brows furrowed together. She didn't like the idea that the police weren't testing everything they could to get to the bottom of crimes.

"The unit we took this off isn't the most honest one they could be. They're renowned for taking the cheap option, especially if it's something expensive," Hadrian admitted.

"You should have heard the assistant pathologist's opinion on the matter when we collected the body," Zack mumbled. "She isn't happy with the situation, but all of their reputations are tarnished now. She has no choice but just to accept it is how it is and carry on working there. Her boss might not be the best with a scalpel, but Diana is good at what she does. She always makes sure the samples are well cared for."

The way he spoke about the other woman had jealousy clawing in Cassie's stomach. And she hated it. The assistant pathologist wasn't in any position to steal Cassie's mate from her, and logically, she knew that. It was hard to remember though.

"Which means they haven't run it through the database yet," Cassie responded. "If it's human then we might have a good place to start."

"If it's human then they're going to be in big trouble," Hadrian growled, his sharper canines glinting in the light and making him appear a little more menacing than he maybe should.

"At least it's somewhere to start," she responded.

"It is. I guess that's what we need to get going. Issac, get in contact with the rest of the units across the country and look into where the facility could be. Cassie, testing is a priority, Zack will help you with whatever you need. I'm going to go and have a chat with the assistant pathologist and hope she remembers even more than she reported at the time."

Everyone nodded, and the shuffle of papers filled the

room as they each prepared to head off and do the work they needed to.

"Let's go catch a murderer," Hadrian announced. "If anyone can do it, I know we can."

Cassie nodded but wasn't quite so convinced. They didn't seem to have a lot to go on, which meant whoever was responsible had a lot of knowledge in how to cover up. Even as inexperienced at chasing down murderers as Cassie was, she knew that meant trouble. And it would almost certainly mean another body. That was something she definitely wanted to avoid. No one deserved the fate of Tyann and the others.

EIGHT

Her eyes widened as she took in the flashing letters on the screen. Human. The DNA was human. Depending on what happened when they ran the DNA profile through the system, this could change everything for them.

But first, she had to check the sample from the other body. If it wasn't a match, their case was somewhat weakened. Though she didn't know exactly what would happen if a human was committing a crime against a paranormal. They weren't supposed to use magic around them or let on that this entire world existed and yet it couldn't just be ignored.

That was probably a decision for the High Council and not for her. Cassie's responsibility was to do her job and help the team get to the bottom of who was doing this. Even at her proper job, the important thing was for her to discover what was going on with the blood, not to do anything about what she found.

She pressed the button to re-run the test, crossing her

fingers and hoping for the best. If they wanted to be able to trace the person doing this, then they needed it to be human. If it wasn't, they were back to square one. Maybe. It would certainly take a lot longer for her to be able to work out what kind of paranormal it belonged to. After that, they'd only be faced with the frustrating possibility of having to persuade whatever Council they belonged to and hand over anyone suspicious.

"Like that's going to happen," she muttered darkly.

"What did you say?" Zack asked from behind his computer.

"Sorry, I was talking to myself." She winced. Why had she let him hear her? He already didn't like her.

"Anything I should know?"

"Not yet. I'm just re-running the test to be sure," she responded.

"What did it say the first time?"

"Human," she whispered.

"It is?" He perked up, suddenly paying a lot more attention.

"The first test said so. I'm just rechecking it to be sure," she replied, pressing the button she needed to.

"Rerunning is good," he said to himself.

Cassie didn't reply. She didn't need to. Both of them knew they needed to be sure of this before they ran the DNA through the human system.

"How are we even going to be able to run the DNA?" she asked, almost in disbelief that she hadn't thought to ask any of them before. Surely it wouldn't be as easy as just walking into the station and asking.

"How much did Hadrian tell you about what he does here?" Zack responded.

"Not a lot." Now she thought about it, she knew

precisely what Zack's position was. And even had a good idea about what Issac did. Hadrian on the other hand...

"He's a computer whiz..."

"A vampire computer whiz?" She turned to face him, raising an eyebrow.

"Oh, I'm sorry, what did you expect him to be? Not all vampires can be historians, you know."

"I don't think it can count as a historian if they lived through it anyway," she muttered.

Zack chuckled. "Don't let any of the vampire historians hear you say that. I don't believe they'll take very kindly to it."

"There actually are some?"

"Of course. You don't really think it was chance they discovered King Tut's tomb, do you?"

"Are you suggesting Howard Carter is a vampire?" She wasn't sure if she believed him or not. Lying about something like that seemed entirely in character with Zack and how he saw her.

"Was," Hadrian interrupted. "Unfortunately, he's not with us any longer. It's a shame, he was a good man."

Cassie's mouth fell open. She knew paranormals were everywhere, she just hadn't considered that some of the names she'd learned about at school might have been them too.

"I'd close your mouth, Cassie, or someone might find a use for it." Zack's voice cut through, making the words less of a joke than they should have been.

There was no mistaking his eyes though. He was watching her in a way that suggested he very much wanted to act on what he'd said.

"Okay, so Howard Carter was a vampire," she said needlessly.

"So are a lot of other people. We tend towards long-lived." Hadrian shrugged as if it wasn't a big deal. She supposed that to him, it wasn't. He'd had a long time to get used to the vampire life. As a witch, her life span was only slightly longer than a human's.

"How old are you?" she blurted, despite knowing it was rude to even think the question, never mind ask.

"How old would you like me to be?" He smirked at her.

"Just tell her. Otherwise, she'll spend more time trying to figure that out than the case," Zack put in.

"I don't know exactly when I was born. I don't even know if I was born a vampire or not. I know I was one by the time I was five or six, so my guess is that I was born not made."

"Why don't you look it up?" she asked.

"There aren't exactly great records from the poor houses at the end of the nineteenth century." He shrugged. "I long ago came to terms with never knowing where I came from."

"So that makes you..."

"I'm about a hundred and thirty. Give or take a couple of years. I'm not completely sure. The date wasn't that important until I worked my way up to work for the police at the time."

"You started as a police officer?"

"You're full of questions today," he observed.

"Just doing my job so I can trust the people I'm working alongside," she pointed out. "You'd be asking me all kinds of questions if you hadn't been stalking me in the first place."

Zack snorted, drawing a withering look from Hadrian.

"You think we stalked you?"

"In a manner. You picked me because of what I am and where I worked. But I reckon there's more to it than that. Besides, it's not like I scream witch."

His eyes raked down her body at that comment, taking in the simple jeans and a shirt comb.

"The hair kind of gives it away."

"Not true," she countered. "A lot of women dye their hair. I just have an easier way of doing it." She pulled the tie from her plait and untangled it before running her hands through the loose strands. Sparks danced over her head, making her hair bubblegum pink.

"Impressive, though I'm not sure I see the point," Zack said.

"There is no point," Cassie responded, trying not to get too annoyed. "I do it because I like how it makes me feel. That's all."

"Women are baffling," the bat shifter moaned.

She was saved from replying by the beeping of the machine. Ignoring the two men, she turned back to it, hoping it was going to give them the answer they all wanted.

"It's human." She sighed with relief. "I'm not even sure if that's good or bad," she added.

"It's good for the case, bad for paranormals," Hadrian responded. "Can you set up a DNA profile for it? Then I'll run it through the system."

"Erm..."

"It's okay, I'll show you how," Zack promised. "It's easy once you've done it the first time."

"Thank you."

"Excellent. Let me know when you've done it." Hadrian didn't wait for either of them to respond and walked straight back out of the room.

"Great, right. That answered all the questions I had."

"And what questions are those?" Zack prompted.

"Never mind. Let's just get this done and then we can go find out if our culprit is on the system."

"Are you hoping he is?"

"Aren't you?"

He didn't answer.

"Look, Zack, I know you don't believe in humans being able to hurt paranormals..."

"That's not what I said."

"Isn't it? You denied the witch hunts." She folded her arms, facing off against him. "So why don't you believe they can hurt paranormals?"

He scowled, something dark crossing across his face. "Of course, they can hurt paranormals."

"Wait, what? That's not what you said before..."

"Just drop it, Cassie," he demanded.

"Why? So you can keep contradicting yourself?"

"My Mum was killed by a human. Alright? She was dating him, and he turned on her. The witch hunts were bad, but don't you dare suggest they're the worst thing a human can do to a paranormal." The pain and hurt sang through his voice and felt like knives in her heart. And not just because she'd pushed him to tell her either. She could feel his terror, his hurt, his loss. Now it made sense why Zack was here. He wanted justice for people that had none.

"Zach..." She held out her hand to touch him, but he stepped back, avoiding her successfully.

"Let's just get this profile done," he insisted, grabbing his laptop. "There's a couple more things you need to do first."

"I know." It had been a long time since she'd done it, but she remembered how from her time at university.

"Then let's get on with it."

She sighed. He clearly wasn't going to tell her more about his Mum's death, even though he seemed to need to talk about it. She tried to remind herself that it wasn't any of her business and that if he ever did need to talk about it, she could make sure she was there for him.

"Let's." She pushed her concerns to the side and prepared to create a DNA profile, knowing it could change everything for their investigation.

NINE

Cassie rubbed her forehead, trying to erase the dizziness from watching so many DNA profiles flash in front of her face.

"You know you don't have to watch them, right?" Issac asked, leaning against the door.

"Yes," she responded. "But I've never seen the process before." And it fascinated her to see how the program lined everything up only to have it disappear seconds later, dismissed for not being the right fit.

"Ah, you're that kind of person."

"I'm what?" She turned to look at him properly.

He looked far too relaxed for the situation they were in. Almost like it didn't matter to him that they were in such a high-pressure situation.

"You're the kind of person who wants to do all this for a love of science. And answers. It's not about the murder, it's about you learning more."

She opened her mouth to argue but closed it again. She couldn't deny that there was an element of truth in what he was saying. It had become more personal with Tyann's death, but she was still mostly motivated by being able to learn more about the processes by which they could catch the killer.

"There's no shame in it, Cassie. In fact, it'll probably serve you well. Sometimes, we can't catch the killer. Sometimes, we fail. And if you're the kind of person doing this for justice, it can hit you hard."

"Like Zack?" she asked, unable to help herself.

Issac chuckled. "Yes, exactly like Zack. And like Hadrian used to be, though I think he grew out of it a few decades back."

"And why are you here?" She knew about the other two, but Issac didn't seem like he fit into either of their motivations.

"By accident. It's hard to get a job as a necromancer sometimes. Even harder to find one that actually uses my magic for good."

"And that's what you're here to do?" she prompted.

Issac shrugged. "Not really. I'm here because Hadrian found me at the Job Centre."

"The Job Centre?" she echoed. "As in..."

"Yes, as in the place humans go when they aren't able to get employment. Believe me, it wasn't my first choice either, but there was nothing else I could do. I needed a job to feed myself, and the only ones available to me were somewhat distasteful in nature. Hadrian was looking for a necromancer who would do what he needed them to and made me an offer I couldn't refuse."

"I hope he didn't take advantage of your situation," she said softly.

"He didn't. And I'm firm enough in my beliefs of how things should be that I wasn't going to compromise just for money. I made him give me assurances that I'd never be asked to raise the dead or use my powers to hurt anyone." He moved further into the room and perched on the desk.

"Why do you stay now?" She wasn't sure what made her ask. But something told her it wasn't because of money or job security.

"Now I stay for the reason you think. There's something euphoric about stopping someone from causing so much harm. I like being a part of that. And it gives me a family."

"You think of Hadrian and Zack as your family?"

"Do you always ask so many questions?" he threw back.

"When I get the chance." She shrugged.

"And you just expect me to answer them?"

"You don't have to. But the fact you haven't told me no suggests you will."

"I thought you were a chemist, not a psychologist," he muttered.

"Can one not be both?" she teased.

"Are you?"

She shook her head. "Just someone that knows people."

"Yes, I see them as my family," he admitted.

She was saved from responding by a beep from the machine. She should start thanking the technology gods for getting her out of awkward conversations, that was the second time in the same day.

"It has a match." She almost couldn't believe it, but the words 'match found' flashed up on the screen. There was no avoiding them. But who could it possibly be?

"I'll get the others." Issac slipped out of the room before she could respond. Not that she'd have contradicted him anyway. The four of them needed to decide what they were doing together.

"Who are you?" she asked the computer screen. A little

part of her was almost scared to press the button and find out. She didn't even know why she felt that way. She knew humans, yes, but not many. And not any that would horrify her if she saw their name as a match for the DNA.

"The machine found a match?" Hadrian asked as he walked in.

"Yes." She gestured toward the beeping machine.

"Have you looked yet?"

She shook her head. "I thought it best to wait."

"Normal people would have looked," Zack muttered.

Cassie glared at him. What was his problem now? She'd thought they'd managed to find some kind of middle ground while working together but it appeared she'd been wrong.

"Well then, let's find out who it is." Hadrian leaned in and pressed the button, revealing the DNA profile of the culprit to them all.

"Michael Riggs," Issac read.

"What?" Cassie blinked a couple of times, not believing what she was seeing. This made no sense.

"You know him?" Zack demanded.

"He's my boss," she whispered. "But this can't be right. This must be a mix-up..." She just couldn't believe that Michael was the one behind everything. She sometimes got a weird feeling from him, she wasn't going to deny that, but that didn't mean he was out there killing paranormals and leaving his DNA all over the place. Besides the fact he didn't seem like the type, he was also a scientist. Surely he wouldn't be stupid enough to leave proof of his crime under his victims' fingernails.

"Your boss?" Issac echoed. "Are you sure?"

"Without seeing a photo, no, but it's his name," she said evenly.

"We can get a photo," Hadrian responded. "Just give

me a second." He clicked on a few buttons, no doubt finding the way to Michael's criminal record.

She wasn't sure she was ready to see this, though at least if her boss really was the culprit, they'd know how they could get him, and that was undoubtedly one of the most significant problems they'd faced up until now. Finding out who did it was hard enough. Finding the person so they could do something about it was a completely different one.

"Here you go." Hadrian pointed at the screen where a criminal record now filled the screen.

Cassie sucked in a breath. There was no doubt the man in the photo was her boss, even if it had been taken when he was much younger. "What's the record for?" she asked softly.

"Animal cruelty," Hadrian responded. "He was only fifteen, so they convicted him as a minor."

"Any jail time?" she asked.

He shook his head. "Mandated therapy and a record."

"I thought these things were supposed to be sealed when the minor turned eighteen?" At least that's what she'd thought was the case.

Hadrian shifted uncomfortably. "The program we use isn't exactly the police one," he admitted.

"And doesn't obey the police rules. Got it." It actually made some kind of sense to her. It was often said that crimes in the youth were linked to crimes once the person was grown. It seemed the stretch from animal to shifter in this case only proved it.

She looked back at the photo, trying to reconcile what was in front of her and what she knew of the man. Had he understood what he was giving her when he gave her the avian shifter blood? He must have. If he was behind this, then he would have recognised whatever had been done to the blood.

"We're in trouble," she whispered.

"What?" Zack snapped.

"That man, he's my boss. He gave me the avian blood you sent to the lab. Which means he knows what it is. And he asked me to test it..."

"Which means that you now being off sick looks suspicious," Hadrian finished.

"Especially if he saw your name on the visitor log," she responded.

"I didn't sign in with my real name."

She let out a sigh of relief. That was something at least, though she didn't feel like it was quite enough to reassure her about the difficult position they were in.

"What if Cassie goes back to work tomorrow?" Issac asked.

"And put her in more danger?" Hadrian demanded.

"One of us can play the part of a visiting doctor?"

Hadrian pursed his lips as he considered that course of action. "Would that work?" he asked her.

She nodded. "We have visitors all the time. Just come in and act like you know what you're doing."

"I'll do it," Zack offered. "At least I'm an actual doctor."

"You finished training?" Cassie's eyes widened before guilt assailed her. She shouldn't doubt his accreditation. Not when she'd watched him do an autopsy already.

"Yes." He didn't look at her as he answered. "It makes the most sense," he added.

"It does," Hadrian admitted. "But I'll need the two of you to stay after hours to do some digging around."

Cassie nodded eagerly. "I'll just say I'm staying late to catch up on the work I'm missing now. It should work."

"Okay, Cassie, Issac will take you home. Zack, take me through what we know about the bodies again. We might be able to find something new now we know the culprit is human."

"I don't need a babysitter to take me home," she protested.

"No, you don't. But given we're pretty sure your boss is behind all of this, I'm not willing to take the risk. One of us will be with you when you're outside your own home."

She tried to find the words to argue but wasn't actually sure she disagreed. It would put her mind at ease to know one of them was close.

"Fine," she accepted eventually. "Let's go," she instructed Issac.

"You got it." His boyish grin was back, no doubt due to being able to spend more time with her. She couldn't say she wasn't pleased too. There was very little she could do to deny the bond between them. Between her and any of the three of them. And she wasn't going to pretend otherwise when she didn't have to.

"I just need to grab my bag from the lab," she told him.

He nodded. "Lead the way."

TEN

"I'll see you later," Issac said as he stood on the threshold of her front door.

"You can come in, if you want," she responded, stepping back so he could see the inside of her flat.

Indecision warred over his face as he tried to decide whether he was going to or not.

"Are you sure?"

She nodded. "I don't have any beer or anything, but I can make a pot of tea for us and have some great biscuits my Mum sent." She really should remember to call her and thank her for the sweet treats. She kept meaning to, but other things got in the way.

Then again, it might be better to hold off until she had mating news for her Mum. Then she wouldn't have to lie when she asked when Cassie planned on settling down.

"That sounds good," Issac responded. "But only if you're certain."

"I am," she returned, almost annoyed that he wasn't just taking her up on the offer. Surely he was supposed to jump every time she wanted to spend time with him. She chided herself for that thought. She shouldn't insist on how people felt around her. Particularly not one of her mates.

"Are you always this tidy?" His eyes trailed over the neatly organised living room.

She gave a short laugh. "I'm not tidy at all. I just have the advantage of having this." She held up her hand and watched as red sparks danced around her fingers.

"Much easier than having to draw blood to do magic," he observed.

"I imagine so." They stared at each other, neither one of them able to break the tension between them. "Tea!" she exclaimed.

"Two sugars? If that's okay?"

"I think I have some, I'm not sure." She turned and headed towards the small kitchen, intent on doing as she'd promised and make tea. All the while hoping she had some sugar left over from the last time she'd done some baking.

"Are you okay with going back to work tomorrow?" Issac leaned against her kitchen door, looking completely at home in her flat. That was something she could get used to, but knew was impractical. With three mates, her flat would quickly become far too small for them, and she wouldn't pretend otherwise.

"No," she admitted as she flicked the kettle on. "I'm terrified. Michael has been my boss for as long as I've been there. He has weird moments, but I can't imagine him doing anything this bad."

"Maybe he didn't?" His voice shook, revealing just how little he believed that.

"I doubt the DNA is lying," she countered. "He did this. And he gave me the blood anyway. Did he want me to work out what it was?"

"Why would he want that?" Issac asked.

"Maybe to trick me into revealing I'm more than just human myself?" She shook even as she considered what that could mean. Would she have ended up being his next victim? As dead and haunted as Tyann was.

Issac stepped forward and wrapped his arms around her, pulling her close and stroking her hair. "It's okay. He can't have known. You never use magic at work, right?"

She shook her head, not ready to leave the comfort of his chest behind. He was so warm. Surprisingly so given the fact he was a death magic being.

"Then it'll be fine. He was probably just putting it through testing to make sure it wasn't possible to identify it."

She shuddered even as Issac stroked her hair soothingly. As much as she wanted to believe what he was saying, a large part of her couldn't. If Michael was capable of doing what he had to Tyann, then he was more than capable of tricking her into revealing what she was and making her his next victim.

"How is he even picking them?" she whispered.

"He's definitely worked with you the whole time?"

She nodded. "Except every couple of months when he goes to some conference or other. He's in the lab most days."

"Conferences?" He leaned back, looking down at her until she met his eyes.

"Yes. To do with the tests and other procedures we do." She frowned, trying to work out what he was getting at. "Why?"

"I'm just wondering if they coincided with when the others disappeared."

Her eyes widened. "Could it be that simple?"

"Do we have any way of finding out?" he asked.

She nodded. "His diary. I'm not sure if it's synced to

the rest of ours, but I can check tomorrow and email you about when he was where."

"Don't email us," he said quickly. "If he is aware of what you are and where you've been today, it's better not to give him any proof."

"Oh." She hadn't thought of that and cursed herself a little for that. She prided herself on her intelligence, and yet here she was not coming to sensible conclusions like that. "Sorry, I don't know what's going on with me."

"It's been a long couple of days. Full of a lot of discoveries."

"You can say that again," she muttered. Just forty-eight hours ago she'd been mate-less and had a stable, if boring, job. Now, both of those had changed. Fate had a strange way of working sometimes.

"And remember, Zack will be with you tomorrow," he murmured.

Zack. Now there was a conundrum. She didn't even know if she was reassured by that or not.

Issac brushed a strand of bubblegum pink hair behind her ear. She licked her lips, hoping he was thinking the same as she was right now. It would be a little embarrassing if he wasn't.

Thankfully, Issac lowered his lips to hers, kissing her softly. He pulled her closer, every movement revealing just how tentative he was about the whole situation. Maybe he felt like he should be waiting for a better moment, or perhaps it was because the other two weren't with them. Whichever it was, she couldn't bring herself to care. Not with the sparks running up and down her body. He might be a necromancer, but he was undoubtedly eliciting feelings of life inside her.

"Wow," she murmured as she pulled back.

"Wow, indeed. I never dreamed it would be like that," he responded.

"Being with me? Or just your mate in general?" she responded, nerves starting to assail her. Had he not felt the same thing she had?

"Mate in general." Issac brushed another strand of hair away, trailing his fingers down her cheek in the process. "I'm a necromancer, we don't really get to think about mates as much as the rest of you."

"What do you mean?" She frowned, but didn't move out of his arms. Not even to deal with the now boiled kettle.

"I'm sure you've heard all of the rumours about my kind."

"Well, yes," she admitted.

"It makes it hard for us to meet people. I long ago resigned myself to not finding my mate easily, potentially ever." He glanced away but not before she'd seen the sadness in his eyes.

"And you didn't think that would change when you joined Hadrian's team?" she asked softly.

"I hoped. But we don't exactly meet a lot of people that aren't dead."

She chuckled and leaned into him more. "That can be a slight hindrance."

"But when we walked in the other night..."

"Everything changed," she answered for him.

"Yes. It really did."

"And you knew in that moment?" She wanted to fidget but couldn't. That was probably for the best, she didn't want him to know just how unsure of herself she was.

"We all knew in that moment, you can't say you didn't either." He smiled knowingly, and she had to admit he was right.

"I didn't know it was all three of you," she admitted. "Just that my mate was in the room."

"Isn't it better this way?" he teased.

"I'm not so sure yet. Three mates feels like a lot of work, and..." she trailed off, unsure how to voice the worry.

"And?"

"Are you just my mates? Or are you each others' mates too?" she whispered.

"I only have the urge to kiss you, if that answers your question."

"Hmm." She wasn't sure how she felt about the potential of them being each others' mates as well as her. Jealous was her first guess, but she pushed it aside. They'd establish how their relationship worked in time.

"Just let things play out like they're supposed to," he suggested. "You'll find things will work out like they should."

"I hope you're right." She sighed, hating how complicated everything seemed to be now.

"I am right," he responded.

"Are you always this cocky?"

"No. I leave that to Hadrian."

"And the miserableness to Zack, no doubt. But what does that make you?" She tried to keep the amusement out of her voice but knew she'd failed.

He chuckled, his whole chest vibrating under her cheek from the sound. "Zack is something else," he responded. "But he'll come around."

"Yes, Hadrian said that." She pulled away from him to make the tea she'd promised.

"You don't believe him?" Issac prodded.

"I'm not sure whether or not I do," she admitted. "I've not seen anything from Zack to suggest he's interested in being anything more than acquaintances."

She poured the water on the tea and pulled out an old bag of sugar. She frowned at the crystals that had formed inside of it. Squeezing it with her hand, she loosened just enough of it to make Issac his tea before abandoning it back in the cupboard.

"Couldn't you just use magic to sweeten it?" he asked, having watched precisely what she was doing.

"I could," she responded. "But it doesn't taste quite the same done that way." She shrugged. It was something a lot of witches learned at an early age. Magic would do in a pinch, but it just wasn't as good as the real thing.

"Ah. I didn't know how it worked."

"I think that's normal," she replied. "I have no idea how necromancy works either." Or shifting for that matter. Everything she knew came from rumours and whispered talk. Not for the first time, it occurred to her that just a little bit of communication could go a long way between different kinds of paranormals.

She added a dash of milk and passed the mug to him.

"Thanks." Their hand brushed again, sending tingles through her.

"Do you ever think that will stop?" she asked, hoping he'd both say yes and no. It wasn't like she wanted the chemistry between them to fade, but it would be a little impractical for her to want to do magic every time she touched him. And even less so if she felt the same every time she touched Zack and Hadrian too. If Zack ever touched her anyway.

"From everything I've heard, it will once we seal the bond. For now, I think it's something we'll have to put up with."

"Seal the bond," she echoed, thinking about what that could end up meaning for her. "How will that even happen?"

"Sex, I assume. You'll need to give your blood to Hadrian and I. Zack will need to bite you. And you'll do whatever it is witches do."

"We spark," she whispered. "It covers our entire bodies and does something that bonds us together." She shrugged. She wasn't entirely sure about the ins and outs of it, but her cousin was mated, and Cassie had asked once when she'd drunk a little too much. She figured it was better to ask than be taken aback when she actually met her mate.

"That sounds like it could be fun." He wiggled his eyebrows.

Cassie chuckled. "I've heard it's a unique experience."

"Then I look forward to finding out. But that won't be for a while."

"You think it'll be awhile until Zack comes around?" A rock dropped in her stomach. She knew what kind of things happened to witches whose mates didn't claim them.

"It won't be as long as you're worrying about."

"You don't know that."

"Not for certain, but I do know Zack, and he's all front. The emotions are bubbling away beneath the surface. He won't let anything hurt you and would protect you with his life." Issac was so sincere she had to believe him.

A laugh caught in her throat. "Though I do believe there is the slight issue of us all dropping over dead if he died."

"I'd just raise you again if that happened."

"I think you'd be dead too..."

"Tomatoes, tomatos," he half-sang. "Let's just make sure none of us ends up in life-threatening situations then."

"You say that like we're not investigating violent crime," she responded.

Issac shrugged. "Live every day like it's your last then. It's the only way you're going to be able to deal with it."

She took a sip from her tea, trying to work out how to respond to that, but she was coming up blank. At least his advice was pretty solid. If she did that, it would be a fun experience.

ELEVEN

Nerves fluttered in her stomach, as they had been all day. No matter what she'd done today, she hadn't been able to get rid of them. It was almost like butterflies had made their home inside her.

And yet nothing had happened. She'd come into work and gone about her day just like usual. Though admittedly with a lot of questions about how she was feeling. At least saying she was still a little under the weather wasn't even a lie.

"How you holding up?" Hadrian asked, perching on her desk as he arrived.

"I'm good," she answered, not even surprised he'd shown up. She'd seen Zack around a couple of times, but he hadn't talked to her.

"Are you sure? Zack said..."

"Zack wouldn't know. I haven't spoken to him all today."

"He's been watching..."

"That's not what you promised," she hissed. She didn't like being the person who called others out, but this needed doing. They'd promised they would keep her safe, especially with her boss about. Never mind the fact they should want it as her mates too.

"He was keeping an eye on Michael," Hadrian responded.

"And?" Her voice changed from annoyed to intrigued in the same word.

"He didn't find much. No mysterious disappearances or tampering with blood samples."

She sighed. "As to be expected," she responded.

"Unfortunately so. Any luck with the calendar?"

She nodded. "I tried to email it to you, but it wouldn't let me without leaving a trace on it." She didn't know much about computers, but she'd worked out that much at least.

"Let me see?"

She knocked the mouse, waking up her computer. After typing in her password, the calendar appeared.

"Great, let me write everything down, and I'll send it on to Issac."

"Alright, just don't get caught."

"Where are you going?" he asked.

"I have results I need to collect from one of the other departments." She stepped away as she said it, only for Hadrian to catch her arm and pull her back.

Without even being sure how it happened, she found her body pressed against his and a searing kiss consuming her. Just like with Issac the night before, sparks threatened to explode from her entire body, and she was sure some probably were. Now she really hoped there was no one around to watch them.

"What did you do that for?" she asked after she'd pulled back.

"Because I wanted to." His voice hoarse from the kiss.

"This doesn't exactly seem like the best place," she half-protested, but both of them knew there wasn't anything in her words. She'd never deny any of them, no matter where they were. She wouldn't want to.

"If we get caught, it might be our only chance for a kiss." He waggled his eyebrows, trying to pull off his comment as a joke. She wasn't fooled.

"Alright. Just keep an eye out for anyone finding you," she cautioned, already wondering what extra sense vampires had and whether he could put them to use now. She wished she could do something to help, but one of the problems with witch magic was that it wasn't invisible. No matter what she did, people would be able to see the sparks she created, and that would lead to questions she wasn't allowed to answer.

"Be back soon." He was already mostly focused on the computer.

She shook her head, a bemused smile spreading across her face. She might not have known them long, but their dedications to their jobs touched her in ways she couldn't explain.

The corridors were mostly empty, no doubt as a result of the fast approaching shift change. She'd always found it a bit like this when the night staff were due in. Hopefully, none of them would ask why she was staying behind. Her sick day had been helpful in that regard. She'd always been a hard worker. People wouldn't think twice about her staying back to catch up on the work she'd yet to do.

Turning into the storage room, she opened the fridge she'd stowed the avian blood in a couple of days before. This wasn't what she'd left Hadrian to do, but something deep inside her had the urge to check whether it was still there. Unsurprisingly, the slot in the rack where the vial should be was empty. She frowned. How had Michael made samples disappear like that?

"I hope you're feeling better," Michael asked.

Cassie jumped. The last thing she'd expected was for him to appear.

"Yes, thank you," she responded, turning around and closing the fridge. Somehow, having the cold metal at her back was reassuring. Though if it would be useful if he tried anything remained to be seen.

"Did you ever finish a report on that blood?" He smiled sweetly at her, but now she knew his true colours, it was hard to see him without thinking about his hands around Tyann's neck. Even if that wasn't how she'd died.

"I did." Her voice shook. The report she'd submitted had been entirely fake, and he likely knew that. She hadn't had any other choice. He was expecting something, and she couldn't submit what she actually knew to be true without causing more problems for herself.

"Oh, I must have missed it. What did you find?"

Was he lying? Or just testing her? It felt almost impossible to tell either way, and she didn't know how to respond to that.

"It was contaminated." She supposed that was the truth, though it didn't stop the nerves which fluttered away in her stomach. She hated lying. Even in situations like this where it was necessary.

"Contaminated?" he echoed, his eyes widening. She had to hand it to him, he was a decent actor. If she hadn't already known his secret, then she didn't think she'd be able to guess he even had one from this conversation.

"Yes. It kept failing all the tests I was trying. It's the only explanation. I'd suggest you ask the person who took the sample in the first place if you want to find out what happened to it," she suggested, trying her best to ignore the question going around in her head about whether or not he'd been the one who took it in the first place. It might not have been. They had no idea how many people were involved behind the scenes, but she doubted he was the only one.

Michael stepped forward, a menacing look flashing through his eyes.

She tried to move backwards, only to be stopped by the fridge that had felt like a safety net just minutes ago.

"Are you sure you don't know what contaminated it?" he asked, crowding into her space.

She wanted to close her eyes but knew she couldn't let him see her fear. It would only encourage him with his intimidation techniques.

"My best guess would be avian blood," she whispered, hoping it wouldn't give too much away. It would be just as bad if he thought she was incompetent at her job. If he wanted to ruin her instead of killing her, he could file a complaint about her falsifying the report. She shook her head. That was a ridiculous thing for her to think about at this point in time. And it hardly mattered anyway, she had three mates to look after her while she looked for another job.

"Avian blood?" Shock covered his features. She'd made a big mistake by admitting that.

He leaned against the fridge, one hand resting to the left of her head. She sucked in a breath, not even daring to breathe properly while he was so close. If he was trying to intimidate her, then he was managing.

"I'd suggest you step away from her."

A sigh of relief left her lips at Hadrian's appearance.

"Excuse me?" Michael sounded about as pissed off as she felt.

"I said, I suggest you step away from her." He didn't

change his tone, but something about the way Hadrian said the words would be intimidating if she didn't know him. Maybe it was something to do with the vampire side of him.

"Who even are you?" Michael demanded, though he stepped back at the same time.

Cassie relaxed slightly, glad to have the room to breathe properly.

"I'm Cassie's boyfriend," Hadrian replied.

A little thrill went through her. While she knew what was between them went far beyond the simple boyfriend-girlfriend classification that humans liked to use, but hearing it made things seem that bit more real.

"I was just catching up with her about a special assignment she was working on."

Cassie suppressed a laugh. He wasn't exactly lying when he said that, she'd give him that.

"Are you done? I promised I'd take her out for dinner. And you know what they say, always keep your woman happy." Hadrian's fake cheeriness was almost sickening, but she knew what he was trying to do.

"I just need to get my bag from my desk first," she told him, hoping it would give them a good excuse to leave Michael far behind.

"No need, I grabbed it when I was looking for you." Hadrian held it up, proving he'd done what he said. "You finished work five minutes ago, right?"

She glanced at her watch before nodding. "Sorry, Michael, I can forward the report to you tomorrow if you've misplaced it." Not waiting for a response, she slipped over to Hadrian and kissed his cheek.

An arm around her shoulders had her instantly feeling more secure, and she leaned into the vampire, enjoying the comfort he was giving.

"Thank you," she whispered once they stepped outside the building. Her heart still pounded harder than she liked, but at least they were safe now. That was something.

"Please tell me you didn't go looking for him?"

"Of course not," she bit out. "I went to see if he'd removed the blood already."

Hadrian paused, causing her to stop walking. "Had he?"

"Yes. I was just about to shut the fridge when he walked in. I'm fairly certain he knows what I am." She shuddered, not wanting to focus too much on the thought if she didn't have to. "You don't think he..."

"No. I think he's more likely to want you as part of his team. He wanted you to test the blood to see what you made of it."

She chuffed. "I'm not so sure about that. Was he human?" She turned to face him as they reached his car.

"You can't tell?" His eyebrows raised further than she'd have thought possible.

She shook her head. "I can only tell when I've spent a lot of time with someone, even then it's patchy." Witches weren't very good at spotting other species. Maybe it was to do with the fact they didn't have to.

"Oh."

"So?" she prompted. "Human? Or something more?" She almost hoped for something more. That way the DNA they'd found would match the wrong guy, and she was looking into it far too deeply. It was wishful thinking, she knew that, but it was worth a try.

"Yes, he's human. There's something off about him, though I can't put my finger on what," he mused.

"Something in his blood?" she asked.

"Just something. He smelled wrong. All of my instincts were telling me not to drink from him."

Her eyes widened. "Okay then..."

"Issac might be able to tell us more..."

"You're not putting him in danger just so we can get answers," she insisted, thinking about how sweet the necromancer had been to her.

Hadrian brushed a finger down her cheek. "Trust me, he's the deadliest of the four of us."

"Four?" she echoed, certain she'd only met three of them.

"Are you not counting yourself?" Amusement coloured his question and she glanced away.

"Yes," she admitted.

"That's okay, we're here to remember you." He placed a finger under her chin and tipped her head back, placing a soft kiss against her lips.

TWELVE

The last thing she'd wanted was to come back into work. Not with Michael knowing what she knew. It just seemed like an unnecessary risk to her. But then, not turning up to work again could also risk Michael trying to find her in other ways.

She jumped as a steamy cup of tea was plonked down next to her hand.

"Issac told me how you liked it," Zack explained.

She spun around, bringing them far closer together than she'd anticipated. "You lot really don't understand the concept of lying low, do you?" she hissed. First Hadrian, now Zack...if she wasn't careful, Michael might see him too and then she'd have to think of another excuse. Somehow, she didn't think the boyfriend explanation would work twice. Or go down well with Zack. He didn't seem to like her at the best of times, she was sure he wouldn't if she was forcing the point about what was between them.

"We're just doing what we promised and making sure you're safe."

"And the tea?" She raised an eyebrow as she leaned

back on her desk, putting a tiny bit of space between them.

"Who doesn't like tea?" He shrugged.

She had to admit he had a point. There was nothing like a freshly brewed cup of tea, and while she wasn't too sure why he'd brought her one, she was grateful for it.

"Thank you." Something lingered between the two of them, but she didn't want to put a name on it. With the other two, it was straight forward. But with Zack...it was better if she didn't think about it too much.

"Alright, I need to get back to doing my fake work." Zack shuffled from side to side but didn't say anything else before disappearing back into the lab. She had no idea what he was doing with his time to make it seem like he belonged there, but this was his second day, and she was reasonably sure he wasn't going to get caught looking suspicious. It helped that they had locums in all the time when other lab technicians were out.

And doctors knew no boundaries. They were always walking in and demanding the lab ran the tests they wanted, the minute they wanted them. It annoyed them all to no end, but there wasn't anything they could do about it.

Turning back to her work, she pulled up the report she'd faked for the avian shifter blood, preparing to send it off to Michael. If she did that, maybe he wouldn't seek her out again, and she'd avoid the same awkward situation she'd encountered the previous day. But she needed to get through the day so they could do some investigating after most people had gone home. There just wasn't any other way for them to get the answers they needed.

Remembering her tea, she picked up the mug and took a sip, enjoying the perfectly brewed drink. Maybe Zack did care, if he didn't want to be her mate, he wouldn't have done something as sweet as that.

She sent the report off, hoping there was nothing too bad in it that would tip him off about what she was. She didn't believe Hadrian was right about Michael wanting her to work for him. She'd end up the same as Tyann if he caught her. Experimented on and then throat slit when there was nothing more useful to get from her. It sucked, but it was true.

Confident she'd done all she could, she went about the rest of her day. Testing blood samples and filling out the various reports she needed to. There was something reassuring about being able to get back to the job she knew by heart, but at the same time, she knew this wasn't a long-term job for her. It never really had been. She wanted something more in life. Something like what she had with the three guys. Looking into the murder was the most interesting thing she'd done in a long time.

She'd tell them when she saw them all later. The last thing she wanted was to debate on the decision and end up waiting too long. Maybe they'd think she didn't want to be part of their team when that was far from true. Working with her mates would be a dream come true. Working to help save lives would be even better than that.

Checking over her shoulder to make sure there'd be no unpleasant surprises. It was the best way to avoid a situation like the day before, especially as she was reasonably sure Hadrian wasn't about to save her today.

She stepped into the storage cupboard, letting the door close swiftly behind her. There was plenty of space in there, and with the light on, there was nothing to worry about. She'd rather have the door closed and not have to worry about someone creeping up on her.

"Cassie? You on your own?"

She jumped at the sound of Zack's voice but relaxed in the next moment.

"What are you doing here?" she asked.

"Where do you think I've been going when I'm not prowling around the lab?" His lopsided grin was so at odds with his usual demeanour that it took her a moment to recognise him.

"I don't know, but doesn't anyone find it fishy that you just materialise out of the cupboard every now and again?" she demanded, unsure how she should be taking that. She didn't even dare point out that it wasn't helping her safety if he was hiding out in a cupboard all day. But then, she'd not thought Zack would be particularly focused on that anyway. Even if her life was part of his now.

"No one's noticed." He shrugged.

"How can you even be sure about that?" She really didn't like how flippant he was about the situation. There was far too much at stake for this.

"Because everyone is so wrapped up in their own jobs and life to even pay me any attention. And also, because I haven't been randomly reappearing from the cupboard in time. I'm a shifter, I did what we do and flew through the air vents to get places."

"Huh." Just the thought of that was an amusing prospect, though her thoughts took a very different direction when she realised that would mean he had to get undressed.

She looked away from him, somewhat uncomfortable about it. He might be her mate, but he didn't feel that way about her, and she didn't want to violate him like that. It wouldn't be fair to him.

"What were you looking for?" he asked. "Maybe I can help you find it?"

"So I can get out of your hair?" she snapped.

"Or so people don't think you're gone long enough to have a tryst in the cupboard," he pointed out. "I'm not sure that's a good career move."

"Like you care," she muttered.

"I do," he whispered. "Of course, I care. It would be stupid of me not to."

"Oh, so you're finally admitting that I'm going to be a part of your life?" She raised an eyebrow, conscious of the closeness forced upon them by the shelving. While the storage room was big enough for one person, two made it seem somewhat crowded.

"Well, you will be, won't you?"

"You don't even like me," she countered.

"That's not true. I find your intelligence very attractive," he responded, an uncharacteristic earnestness in his voice.

"You're my mate, you're biologically required to be attracted to me." And him saying the words to her didn't help. She didn't want mates that didn't want her for her. Though she knew it wasn't how mating worked, it didn't change her desires.

"Attracted, yes. Maybe even for no reason. But that's not what I said. I find your intelligence attractive, Cassie. Not because I have to, or because the bond between the two of us says I should. I really do find you attractive. Especially when you think no one is watching and you chew on your bottom lip while looking into your microscope..."

"Oh." She had nothing else to say, not when they were as close as they were.

His breath fanned against her cheek as he spoke, sending small thrills through her.

"Believe me, Cassie, what I feel for you is real." He reached out and cupped her cheek in his hand.

"I..."

"Don't need to say anything," he whispered.

Zack slipped his arm around her waist, pulling her closer to him. Not that she was difficult to convince. His lips met hers, igniting the sparks under her skin that had just been waiting to be set free. She'd been starting to worry that Hadrian was wrong about Zack also being her mate, even if it made complete sense given the way she felt around him.

A scratching at the door distracted her from the press of Zack's lips against hers and she pulled away, her eyes wide.

"What was that?" she demanded.

"I don't know."

"You haven't seen any rodents in here, have you?" She scanned the floor, looking for any sign of mice or rats. It would be an easy explanation for what she'd just heard.

"Unfortunately not, I've been a bit peckish, a mouse would have taken the edge off."

Her mouth fell open. Was he serious?

"What?" She blinked a couple of times, still not quite believing what he'd said.

"It's only like a vampire drinking blood," he countered.

"I thought bats ate insects."

"Depends on the size of the bat." He shrugged. "I assure you, I'm big enough to eat a mouse."

"And you would?"

"Is that really what you want to focus on right now?"

"Yes. It saves me from checking the door," she whispered.

He smoothed a hand up and down her arm, offering her the comfort she sorely needed. The moment he let go, she felt his absence. She hated the mating bond right now more than ever. It changed her from an intelligent woman to what felt like a simpering fool.

He rested his hand against the handle and pushed down on it. The door rattled in the frame, but nothing more happened.

Cassie closed her eyes, trying to regain her focus.

"Can you use magic to unlock it?" he asked.

"I can try." Her voice shook as she responded. She'd have preferred not to use magic here at all. She tried to keep her job and her witchiness as separate as possible in case the wrong person saw.

Creeping up to the door, and not knowing why, she brought her magic to her fingertips, the red sparks dancing over her hand. She sent it towards the handle, instructing it to unlock with her mind. Slowly, she tried to open it, only to discover the same thing as before.

"Someone's spelled it." That was concerning, especially as she didn't know how it could even be possible. As far as she knew, she was the only witch that worked in the lab, or any of the others associated with it.

"Can you recognise the magic?" Zack asked, standing behind her.

"No. It doesn't seem to have one profile at all." She felt around with her magic, trying to find out as much as she could about the magical lock around the door and coming up blank. "It's almost like it's a mix of several witches' magic." Something she'd only seen once or twice in her life. Most witches didn't do magic with others. It was something extremely personal to them and not to be shared. Exactly like their familiars.

"Riz..." she whispered.

"My name is Zack." He sounded confused, but she ignored it.

"Riz?" she called louder, hoping her familiar wouldn't

decide this was the moment to be shy. She'd heard that she would appear in front of Cassie's mates, but the creature hadn't done that at any point yet.

"Who..."

He didn't get to finish his question, mostly because of the flickering bat made of red sparks that had appeared in front of his face.

"Zack, Riz, Riz, Zack." She swung her hand between the two of them, hoping the shifter would keep his questions for later.

"Riz, I need you to check the lock, can you get through?" she asked.

The familiar made a motion she'd always interpreted as a nod and shot off towards the door.

"What is that?"

"My familiar," she responded. "Every witch has one."

"I've never seen one before." His gaze was fixated on the glowing red bat in front of him.

"And you won't see another. They only appear for the witch they're bonded to and their mates." She was only half paying attention to him, more interested by any progress Riz might be making.

"This is normal for witches?"

"Of course. We all have one."

"And they're all bats?"

"What?"

Riz backed away from the door, looking at it with an oddly quizzical expression before diving back in.

"Are all the familiars bats?" Zack repeated his question.

She shook her head. "They take on the shape of a witch's mate if they're a shifter, or something else that represents the mate if they're not."

"And if it's two witches who mate?"

"You're full of questions considering we're locked in a cupboard."

"You can talk. You're always asking questions," he threw back.

"That's what is going to make me a good addition to your team." She blanched as she realised what she'd said. She hadn't intended to tell him quite like this.

"Hadrian got to you, then," he said sadly.

"What? No. Hadrian had nothing to do with the decision."

"Then why are you giving up your career here?" he prodded.

"Can we not talk about this right now? I think we have more important things to worry about." Like being stuck with no idea if it was by accident or if it was more malicious than that.

"Right, sorry. Focus on the task at hand."

Riz tried at the door again but didn't seem to be having any more luck than either of them had.

"Eurgh, why can't we open the damn door?" she muttered, trying it once again.

"Because someone doesn't want us to?"

"We don't even know that anyone knows we're in here. Did you bring your phone?" A sudden idea sprung to mind.

"Yes. You don't?"

"No, it's in my bag." She grimaced, feeling like a fool for not bringing it with her, but she never needed it at work and didn't want it to get damaged.

He dug around in his pocket and pulled his out, handing it to her.

"You're just going to trust me with it?" That surprised her and went against everything she'd experienced with him, even if he'd kissed her earlier.

"It's not like you can run off and take nudes with it."

"Don't be crass." She unlocked it and searched for Hadrian's number, noting just how empty Zack's contact list was in the process. Hadrian and Issac were there, as were what appeared to be his dad, but that was it.

Ignoring the lack of people in Zack's life, she pressed the green key to call Hadrian and hopefully get them out of there. Riz fluttered around them, apparently not at all bothered by the lack of freedom.

The phone beeped, making her curse. "No signal."

"I guess no one needs it in a cupboard," Zack deadpanned.

"No, I don't suppose they do," she muttered. "That's a design flaw."

"For an empty room?"

"For anywhere people can get stuck." Frustration rose within her, and she narrowly avoided the temptation of throwing his phone across the room.

"Pass me my phone please?"

"Why?" she asked, even as she handed it to him.

"I'm going to text Hadrian, then it will go through on the off chance we get a sliver of signal." He was typing before he'd even finished talking.

Cassie grunted and found the only patch of wall not covered in shelving. She leaned against it and slid down to the floor, wrapping her arms around her knees and pulling her legs to her chest.

"It could be worse, we could be stuck in a walk-in freezer," Zack quipped as he slid his phone back into his pocket.

She looked up at him, a grimace of disbelief all over her face. Was he serious?

"I got locked in one as a teenager. Worst half an hour of my life," he carried on.

"You got locked in a walk-in freezer?" She couldn't believe this, though had to admit it was lifting her spirits.

"You've met me," he responded.

"They did it on purpose, didn't they?"

"Of course. Apparently, I annoyed them a little bit too much." He flashed her a nervous smile, and she responded with a weak one of her own.

Maybe the two of them were getting somewhere in their relationship. At least, she hoped that was the case. It seemed about right that they'd get there by being locked someplace together. If it had been anywhere but her lab, she'd even have suspected that Hadrian and Issac were behind it. Unfortunately, she doubted that was the case.

THIRTEEN

Cassie rested her head against her hands, at a loss for what else she could do. It felt like they'd tried everything to get out of there. Zack had even shifted and tried to use the air vents, but he'd found a wire mesh stopping him. Something that only concerned her further. If he'd been using the vents all day, like he'd said, then the only reason it would suddenly be blocked was if someone knew what he'd been doing and had blocked it for this exact reason.

It was making the likelihood of an accidental lock in less and less likely by the second.

"Are you sure the text went through?" she asked for what felt like the hundredth time.

"It says it did." She had to hand it to Zack, he was remaining surprisingly patient with her repeated question.

"Then where is he?" she muttered, not expecting an answer.

"He might not have got it yet," Zack responded all the same.

Her breathing grew heavier. She focused on it, trying

not to let the panic of the moment get the better of her. That wouldn't help anyone.

"Can you just blow a hole in the wall?"

She snorted. "I could, but it would cause more damage to us than to the building. We'd certainly be found."

"Damn."

"Yep." There really wasn't any way they were getting out unless Hadrian and Issac turned up and used the key from the outside.

They lulled into an uneasy silence. Each lost in thought. It was a shame being locked in had destroyed the delicious tension the two of them had managed to enjoy just after their kiss. She'd have done anything to have that back.

"Zack..." she started, only to be interrupted by a scratch in the lock.

She jumped to her feet, sparks rising to her hands as she prepared to take on whoever was on the other side. Zack changed his stance, clearly getting ready to fight in his own way. It was a shame his shifted form was so small in situations like this. Though if he was able to eat mice, maybe it wasn't as minuscule as she first thought.

The door swung open, revealing a harried-looking Hadrian on the other side. "Oh, thank the gods," he murmured, rushing forward and pulling Cassie into his arms.

"What took you so long?" Zack accused, though the relief in his voice took away the sting of his words.

"I was with Issac, we think we found where Michael has been keeping the paranormals."

Cassie untangled herself from his arms and gave him a disbelieving look.

"How?"

"Exactly what you suggested. We cross-referenced

when Michael left to go to one of his conferences, and where he claimed to be, and came up with three possible places for the lab."

"And how did you work out which one was the answer?" Zack asked, genuine amusement colouring his tone.

"We followed him."

"Hence why it took you so long to come and get us," Cassie supplied.

Hadrian nodded. "I'm sorry..."

"You can make it up to me later. But for now, let's go."

"Go?" Hadrian echoed.

"Back to the facility you found? We can't just let them get away with it."

The two men exchanged worried glances. Cassie grunted before storming out of the storage cupboard and towards the car park. She just hoped Hadrian had parked somewhere obvious. If he had, she could hotwire his car with magic. That would teach him to ignore it when people were in danger.

"Cassie, wait up," he called. His footsteps thudded on the floor as he caught up with her. She was actually surprised at how far she'd managed to go in such a short amount of time.

"Changed your mind?" she spat out, angrier than she'd actually realised.

"I'm sorry, we shouldn't have hesitated..."

"No, you shouldn't have. Lives are on the line, Hadrian, we can't just sit around and do nothing because the timing isn't quite right for us."

"I know..."

"But?" She spun around and raised an eyebrow, briefly wondering where Zack had gotten to.

"There are protocols we need to abide by."

"Protocols?" She tried not to shout, but she didn't manage very well. Hopefully, none of the night workers were paying any attention to this particular corridor. She doubted it. Unless there was a real emergency, they wouldn't really be doing much. It was one of the best and worst things about the night shift.

"Of course. I'm sure you're familiar with them."

"But why? Don't you have the High Council's permission to do anything?" She frowned, trying to reconcile what he was saying with what he'd told her before.

"Not quite. We work for the High Council, but we're part of a sub-organisation. They set it up after everything with the necromancers happened."

"Sub-organisation?" she echoed, before folding her arms across her chest. "Why didn't you tell me this before?"

"It wasn't important."

"It wasn't?" she squeaked. "I was on the verge of telling you I wanted to quit my job and work with the three of you. But if you're just some part of a bigger organisation, I can't do that, can I?" Tears threatened at the corners of her eyes, but she ignored them.

"Cassie..." He reached out a hand, but she stepped back, stopping him from touching her.

"What's your organisation called?" she demanded. "And what do they actually do."

"We're the PCI."

She gave him a blank look. How was she supposed to know what the random initials he was spurting meant? That wasn't how abbreviations were supposed to work.

"He means the Paranormal Criminal Investigations Department," Zack supplied, slightly out of breath as he handed Cassie her bag.

"Thank you." She'd actually forgotten about it, despite

being so concerned with its whereabouts while they'd been locked in the cupboard. Her phone was less important now. "So, the PCI?" she prompted. They really needed to start giving her better answers, especially as she was stuck with them regardless of how they answered her questions.

"We investigate situations like this one and bring the culprits to justice. Though it's a bit hazier when the guilty party is a human." Hadrian grimaced.

"I can imagine. So, what do we do about this? Lives are at risk, we can't wait any longer." She wasn't going to back down on that. There'd already been four dead bodies, as far as she knew, there could be another one just around the corner if they didn't stop that from happening. Not acting was not an option.

"We can make some calls," Zack responded.

"Great. Hand me the keys." She held out her hand to Hadrian, expecting him to place the car keys in her hand without another word.

"I'm sorry?" His eyes widened, as if he understood what she was asking, but didn't want to admit it out loud.

"The car keys. Hand them to me, please." She made a come-hither moment with her fingers.

To her surprise, Hadrian handed them over.

"Great. Now let's get going."

"It's not as easy as that," Zack protested.

"Then start making calls."

Hadrian sighed and pulled out his phone even as she started walking down the corridor. Now she had Hadrian's keys, things would be a lot easier. It had been a long time since her Dad taught her how to start a car with magic and she wasn't entirely sure she'd have been able to pull it off. He probably wouldn't be happy to learn she'd almost used the skill he taught to steal, but what he didn't know, wouldn't hurt him.

"Hello, Richard? It's Hadrian..."

She zoned out from what he was saying. She didn't need to know what kind of strings he was pulling to make this happen. Just the fact that he was doing it in the first place was enough to her. It proved he was serious about what he was doing. About the fact his job to save people was important.

"You don't need to guilt him into this, you know." The accusation in Zack's tone was difficult to ignore, but she tried anyway.

"Would we be on our way to save lives if I hadn't?" she snapped.

"It's not always about..."

"Not always about protecting people?" She couldn't believe what she was hearing. He couldn't possibly believe what he was saying, could it.

Zack sighed and ran a hand over his face. "Look, Cassie, I'm sorry. I do believe in helping people, I'm not sure what it is about what's going on that's making me into an ass, but..."

"Apology accepted. So long as you're going to help."

"Of course, I'm going to help," he countered. "I haven't run away yet, have I?"

"Doesn't mean you won't," she muttered.

"This is why I work with dead bodies. They're way less complicated to deal with," he muttered to himself.

"And less likely to talk back," she put in.

"That too." He gave a dry chuckle. "I like your wit as well as your intelligence."

"The two often come hand in hand. But if you're not careful, you might actually end up loving me."

They passed through the front doors as they talked and out into the street, Hadrian trailing behind, still on the phone.

"Where did he park?" she asked, looking around the empty lot.

"I've been with you all day, how would I know." Zack shrugged, and she had to admit that he had a point this time.

She turned to Hadrian and gestured to the lack of cars. He pointed to the left and around the corner. Hopefully meaning that was where it lurked.

"Am I even insured on his car?" she mused. She didn't have a vehicle of her own, so her non-existent insurance definitely wouldn't cut it. At this point, she was just grateful she knew how to drive at all and wouldn't just be risking their lives by getting behind the wheel.

"If we crash, you can fix it with magic. Problem solved."

"I suppose that's true." Though if they crashed into someone else, that could be more problematic. "What if we're caught by the police?"

"Then we let Hadrian at them. He can do the weird vampire-hypno thing and they'll forget they saw anything at all."

They turned around the corner and she was relieved to see Hadrian's car sitting in a spot, ready for them.

Her mouth fell open. "That's real?" She'd heard rumours about older vampires being able to control people with their eyes, but had never known whether there was any truth behind them or not. She needed to stop assuming things were made up, she kept getting told she was right about the things she suspected.

"Yes, it's real. I've seen him do it," Zack responded. "Though he doesn't like it. Not a lot of them do from what he's said."

"I get that. It's an invasion of the other person's

consent." She unlocked the car, relieved when it beeped and flashed.

Climbing into the driver's side, she slotted the key in and started the engine as the two men got in.

Hadrian was still talking away into the phone, sounding somewhat frustrated. "I want to talk to Jeanie," he insisted. "Yes, I know it's after hours, but there are lives at stake, and I won't risk them even if that means she has to answer the phone to me."

"Where to?" Cassie mouthed to him.

He pulled the phone away from his ear and put a hand over the microphone. "Look in the sat nav, it's the top location."

"Thanks." She turned back to the car and woke up the navigation device, leaving him to get on with his conversation.

"Jeanie, thank you for talking to me. I need you to authorise a raid for me." He paused, probably to let her respond. "Yes, I know it's unorthodox, but I think there are paranormal lives at stake. We have four dead bodies already and a match to a human man."

Shouting came down the phone, but Cassie knew better than to let it distract her. They needed to get on the road, and that wouldn't happen without her paying attention to the road.

"Turn left at the end of the road," the sat nav's mechanical voice instructed.

"That's going to get annoying fast," Zack muttered.

Hadrian tapped him on the shoulder. "Get Issac on the phone and get him to brief you on what to expect," he instructed. "Yes, Jeanie, sorry I was listening. We did submit a report, but things escalated to a point we couldn't ignore. He assaulted one of our team members, Cassandra Morgan..."

Her heart did a little flutter, surprised that he thought of her as part of his team. She squashed it down as soon as she recalled how he'd said they were part of a bigger organisation. She couldn't just decide to be part of his team. That wasn't how it worked.

"...and then he locked her and Zachary Bolton in a cupboard. I think that constitutes an act of aggression against paranormals. Never mind the fact he has caused the deaths of at least two others. We suspect two more, but we're yet to find DNA evidence linking him to the crimes. Once we're at the facility and have him in custody, I expect we'll find more evidence to link him to those two."

She pulled to a stop at a red light, waiting impatiently for it to change so they could be on their way.

"Understood. We will abide by the rule and only break it if there is an immediate risk to life. Thank you, Jeanie. You'll have my full report by the end of the week." A relieved sigh revealed he'd finally hung up the phone.

"We've got the all clear?" Zack asked.

"Yes. For now. Just get Issac on the phone, we need to prepare for what's happening once we get there."

"That bad?" Cassie asked.

"It's an abandoned warehouse. Not one he owns, but the company went into administration two years ago."

She sucked in a deep breath. "Is that how long he's been doing this?"

"No idea. We have no proof either way, just the recent bodies. I suspect we'll find out more once we've apprehended him."

Zack's hand rested on her leg, the warmth giving her a surprising amount of comfort given the person the hand belonged to. "He'll have needed time to set everything up. I doubt he's been killing people for two years."

"Because you'd have noticed sooner?" She hit the indicator to turn down a country lane, slightly confused about why the sat nav was taking her off the main road already but trusting it to do its job.

"Hopefully," Hadrian muttered.

"There haven't been any other bodies reported that follow the same MO, I don't think he's killed before this."

"But that doesn't mean he wasn't elsewhere." Even in another country, though she didn't voice that opinion. Michael had been her boss for a long time, it didn't seem likely that he'd been sneaking off to foreign countries regularly.

"How long is it going to take us to get there?" she asked, focusing on the road and trying to ignore the macabre direction her thoughts had taken.

"About an hour. He did a good job at managing to find somewhere far enough away not to raise suspicion, but easy enough to get there quickly if something went wrong. It's the kind of place I'd have chosen," Hadrian told them.

"Have you never been tempted to the dark side?" she asked, almost scared of the answer.

"No. Being a vampire isn't all about blood lust like people think. It's surprisingly easy to keep my mind off blood and on whatever job is at hand."

"You don't want to drink blood?" She frowned, but kept her eyes on the road, coming to a roundabout and heading towards a motorway. Clearly, the back roads had been a shortcut of some kind.

"Of course I do. I have to drink blood a couple of times a week. But I don't get the urge to drink someone dry. Even at my hungriest. It just sounds messy."

"If you ever get the urge, tell us, and we'll get you an adult-sized bib," Cassie suggested, holding back a laugh.

"And we'll have Issac on standby to bring them back to life after," Zack added, just as amused.

"The two of you are unbelievable," Hadrian muttered, clearly not finding it as funny as they did. "Have you managed to get hold of Issac yet?"

"No," Zack answered more seriously. "But I'll keep trying."

"Good. We need to find out what's happened since I've been gone."

A sense of foreboding came over Cassie. She might not have known them long, but they were her mates, and she wanted them to be safe. More than that, she needed them to be safe. Then they could all get to know each other better and form the bonds they needed to.

FOURTEEN

Gravel crunched as they finally drew up to the front of the warehouse. Much to Cassie's relief, Issac was standing where he said he would be when he'd finally picked up the phone.

She jumped out the car the moment she'd turned the engine off, her feet crunching on the gravel. She winced. Hopefully, no one inside was listening for intruders, and they hadn't realised they'd arrived.

"Alright, what's the plan?" she asked as the three men huddled around her.

"We're not allowed to use any kind of magic unless we have to. Any humans we find are to be captured without it," Hadrian instructed.

Cassie started to grumble, but he held up a hand.

"There's nothing we can do about it, that's the condition of us having permission to even be here. You want to help the people in there, you shut up and do as we've been told."

His words stung, but she didn't protest.

"Can you turn your hair back to its natural shade?"

Issac asked, eyeing up the bright pink that even shone in the darkness.

"Yes." Without waiting, she lifted her hands and ran them through her hair, letting the red sparks fly through it. Soft brown waves fell past her shoulders, unusually dull for her taste, but she'd be able to change it back once they were done. Not being recognised straight away by Michael was worth going without bright hair for a few hours.

"Alright. We know of one main door, so I suspect the best course of action is for Issac to walk straight up to it..."

"Why him?" Zack demanded, clearly insulted that the vampire hadn't selected him for the dangerous mission.

"Because he's the only one that hasn't spent time at Cassie's lab. There's less risk of him being recognised," Hadrian explained, a surprising amount of patience in his voice. He must have spent the rest of the drive planning this, which explained why he'd been so quiet.

"Alright, after Issac is in..." Cassie prompted, hoping to avoid any more showing off from the men. This wasn't the time for who was bravest.

"He'll signal whether it's safe for the rest of us to come in. If it isn't, we'll have to find a fire exit and make our way in there."

"I did manage to get hold of some basic blueprints," Issac put in, already pulling them up on his tablet and showing them. "They're out of date by at least two years, but they should at least give us a good idea of where the entry points are."

"That looks like a potential one." Cassie pointed to an entrance that seemed isolated from any of the others. If they were splitting personnel inside, then that was the one likely to be left unstaffed. "Do we know how many people are inside?" That would help them determine how useful the blueprints would be.

Issac shook his head. "No one's gone in or out since we saw Michael arrive. I haven't seen any other cars parked around either."

"What about life lights?" Hadrian asked. "Can you sense any?"

The necromancer shook his head. "I'm not sure why. It's almost like something is stopping them from showing up to me."

"He's prepared against necromancers?" Hadrian's eyes widened. "This might be more difficult to do without using magic. But we'll find a way."

"Is there a chance there really isn't anyone in there but Michael?" she asked softly, glancing at the imposing grey building to their side. Just the thought of how it must have appeared to Tyann and the others was making her uneasy. It must have been horrifying to be trapped within its metal walls.

"It's possible he's the only one, but somehow, I doubt it. He held at least four paranormals captive, potentially at the same time. He had help from at least one person," Hadrian responded.

"Could Cassie be right?"

The two men turned to look at Zack, apparently as confused as she was.

"Right about what?" she prompted.

"Could this be a new ploy by the witch hunters? I heard they were active last year..." he trailed off, a guilty flash across his eyes telling her all she needed to know. He felt bad about how dismissive he'd been. And so he should.

"I don't think that was a particularly organised branch," Hadrian pointed out.

Cassie nodded. "Our Council put out a warning about them. They're dangerous, but they're not overly organised. One of their facilities was blown up last year and they found a lot of evidence that they were small in number and were very isolated from any other known branches." She shrugged at the bewildered look on their faces. "Basically, stay away from their known location and you're fine."

"Besides, none of the victims have been witches," Issac added.

"Though I did see some similarities to witch blood in their samples," Cassie mused. "Maybe there's something in that?"

"Are you suggesting they're trying to tamper with paranormal biology?" Issac asked.

"I have no idea. We all know it doesn't work like that. The only way our powers can change is if we mate." She'd have to ask them all for blood samples when they got back so she could compare them. If she'd thought about it sooner, she could have had pre-mating samples from them too. But that would have been too perfect. Blood from others of their species should do the trick.

"Alright, so we need to be careful with any of the equipment we find. If in doubt, leave it alone and don't touch it at all," Hadrian instructed.

"Let's just get going before we all lose our nerve," Zack responded under his breath.

"Alright then. Issac, you're up."

The necromancer split from the rest of them and sauntered up to what appeared to be the entrance while they hid to the side. They'd been talking quietly and been shadowed by the building, hopefully keeping them from the eyes and ears of anyone watching for intruders. Cassie certainly hoped that was the case. Being nowhere near as experienced at this as the other three, she had no choice but the trust their judgement on the matter.

Issac pushed on the door, only to step back and glare at

it. Cassie started to move, determined to help him and unlock it with her magic.

A firm hand on her shoulder pulled her back. "He doesn't need help," Zack whispered.

She watched in awe as Issac cut himself, purple smoke rising from the wound and moving towards the door on his command. Even having seen necromancer magic before, she was amazed. There was something beautiful about it. And dangerous. No wonder most of the paranormal community was terrified of the whole species. They could do a whole lot with that power.

The smoke faded away and Issac pushed the door again, opening for him this time. He disappeared for a moment, no doubt checking what he had to. A few minutes later, his head popped around the door and motioned for them to come with him.

The coast must be clear. The three of them crept forward, none of them making any more noise than they had to. If this was going to become her new norm, then Cassie was going to need some different shoes. The ones she was wearing didn't feel nearly sturdy or sneaky enough for covert missions. And maybe some new clothes too. Some that would make her feel as if she could fade into the background a little bit more. When she'd gotten dressed this morning, she hadn't expected that she'd be here.

"The lighting is very dim, careful where you tread," Issac whispered as they reached him.

They nodded and set off down the corridor. With no one else around, the whole place was eerily quiet and filled with a sense of foreboding. She just hoped the light had been better when the poor captives had been brought in. The last moments of their lives must have been truly horrifying if this is where they'd taken place. She'd have given anything to take that horror away from them.

A fork in the path pulled them up short, but without saying anything, Hadrian indicated for them to split up.

Cassie moved off to the left with Issac, setting off down the just as gloomy second corridor. It wasn't as open plan as she'd expected a warehouse to be, but maybe that was because they weren't very far in yet. Or perhaps it was due to changes Michael had made to the structure. She had to wonder how much he'd done to make this place perfect to him. The location would certainly stop anyone from investigating on the off-chance, but she was sure he'd had to change other things about it.

She jumped, running into Issac as something clanged. He put an arm around her and squeezed her tightly, sending through as much reassurance as he could. She took all of it. Needing something in the darkness.

Lights flickered up ahead. Her eyes widened. Issac pulled her into a crevice to wait out whatever was happening, but that didn't help her to release the breath she was holding. This whole situation was terrifying, and she had no idea what she was truly facing yet.

After a few moments of tense silence, the two of them breathed out.

"Should we go investigate?" she whispered, hoping her voice wasn't as shaky as it sounded to her. She didn't want him to think she was weak. She didn't want any of them to think that. She could hold her own, even if she had to prove it several times over to everyone. Herself included.

"If we don't want to spend the entire night here, then I suggest so."

"No need to be a smart ass," she retorted.

"Sorry. I hate stakeouts, it makes me grumpy," he admitted sheepishly.

"I thought that was Zack's job?" she asked sweetly, receiving the smile she'd hoped for.

Issac kissed her forehead before slipping back out into the corridor. "Being grumpy isn't his job, it's just who he is."

She followed him out, not responding to his words. Not only did they not warrant it, but she figured it was better if they stayed quiet as much as possible. It had been a mistake to even talk as much as they had so far.

The lights flickered overhead. She tried not to flinch. It was undoubtedly more off-putting than she'd have liked.

"Just take a deep breath," Issac instructed, his voice low.

She nodded, but wasn't sure how to do what he instructed without completely freaking out. She didn't want to be the reason their mission failed, but she also couldn't focus properly without worrying about what they were going to find. There was a reason she'd gone to work in a lab and not a more adventurous field in the first place.

"You just need to hope for the best," he added, brushing a hand over her back. She leaned into him, enjoying the touch and the small amount of comfort it provided. Even if it was fleeting.

"Thanks."

A crash from up ahead stopped her from saying any more, and the two of them exchanged worried glances. Whatever that had been, it wasn't a good sign.

Neither of them said anything as they sped down the corridor, all caution flying out of the window. There was a chance that the crash was someone getting hurt, and she wasn't okay with that risk. Thankfully, it seemed like Issac wasn't either. It was reassuring to know her mates had the same kind of ethics as she did. It would make things a lot simpler if they did end up working together properly.

Turning the corner, she ground to a halt, her mouth gaping at the cells in front of her. All of them were filthy and covered in rust. Given what Hadrian had told them earlier, it seemed like the rust was purposeful. Almost like it was an additional punishment.

"Help me," a strained voice croaked. A hand reached through the bars at the other end.

Cassie stood frozen in horror, unable to properly comprehend what they were looking at. Thankfully, Issac was faster to respond and rushed to the woman. He handed her a flask from his belt, and she took it, greedily downing the water.

"Is there anyone else here?" Issac asked.

"Not in the cells," the woman croaked. "They're all gone."

"Where?" he asked.

"Gone. Gone. Gone. Screams and gone."

A shiver travelled through her. That couldn't have been a good experience for the woman, or for any of the other people trapped here.

"What did they do to you?" Issac asked.

Another crash finally brought Cassie out of her trance. "Not here," she hissed. "Let's get her back to the car."

Issac nodded. As he withdrew his athame, the woman flinched, clearly thinking he was a threat to her. Sadness washed through her as she thought about what that could mean.

"It's okay," Cassie reassured the woman, stepping forward and towards the bars, even if she didn't want to. "We're not going to hurt you. Issac is just going to use his magic to get you out of here." Even as she said it, she found herself wondering if the woman was even a paranormal. They weren't supposed to be using magic in front of her if she wasn't.

116

"Shifter," Issac whispered. "Distract her."

"My name's Cassie," she said, doing as Issac had asked. "What's your name?"

"Kamali." The woman sniffed and wiped her nose with the bottom of her sleeve. "My mate calls me Mali." A sob escaped from her.

"It's okay, we're going to get you out of here and back to him."

The woman nodded but didn't look any less scared. "Where will you take me?"

"We'll need to take you to our headquarters, there we'll be able to give you a checkup. We'll need to take some blood."

The woman's eyes widened, fear filling them in a way Cassie had never seen before.

"I promise we'll talk you through everything we do. But we can't stop the man that did this without your help." Beside her, Issac started to hum, purple smoke rising to greet the bars.

"Promise you'll keep me safe," Kamali begged.

"Of course." Cassie reached through the bars and held the woman's hand, hoping it gave her the comfort she needed.

The metal clanged as the bars fell to the floor, making both of them flinch.

"We need to get going," Issac insisted. "If there's anyone around, they'll have heard that."

"How many people were doing tests on you?" Cassie asked the shifter as she helped her to her feet.

"Three," she whispered. "One man and two women. The women always looked scared. Like they were forced to be here too."

Cassie nodded. "Okay. We'll see what we can do about finding them too." She exchanged looks with Issac, and he pulled out his phone, hopefully, to contact the other two and let them in on what they'd found out and what they were going to do next.

"Can you walk?" Issac asked the woman.

She nodded. "With help."

"Good, let's get you to safety," he responded.

FIFTEEN

Cassie paced back and forth, worrying about everything from the shifter now seated in the back of the car, to her missing mates. Issac had gone back inside to help twenty minutes ago, reasoning that he was the one with the most experience, and she was the one who was least likely to freak out poor Kamali. She had to admit he was right on both of those accounts.

But that meant she was stuck outside with absolutely no idea of what was going on inside or what she could do to help her team. Kamali had fallen asleep now she was tucked up in a blanket and had eaten something, and the last thing Cassie wanted to do was disturb her. Even to check on the woman's injuries. If Zack had been with her, it might have been different. He might be a pathologist, but as a doctor, he'd do a pretty good job of patching a live person up if he needed to.

The doors swung open with a loud bang. Sparks sprang to Cassie's fingertips, eager to be let loose and defend her. It had always amazed her how magic seemed to act like that. It knew she was in danger even before she was.

Except in the storage cupboard, though maybe that was something to do with Zack's closeness confusing it.

"Cassie," Issac called. "Can you help us?"

She didn't wait to respond, but rushed in the direction of his voice. He appeared to be struggling under the weight of two women. Presumably the ones Kamali had told them about. One look told Cassie all she needed to know. These women weren't here voluntarily.

"I need you to check them over while I call for reinforcements."

"That bad?" Her eyes widened.

"They're both human, it's not up to us to deal with them but we can't leave them to the human police. We'll need to call in one of the other departments to take control of Michael too." He glanced over his shoulder, but she couldn't work out at what.

"Are they okay?" she whispered, meaning the two women he was carefully propping up against the side of the building.

"They should be. I think they're malnourished and might have some superficial scratches, but nothing too serious. Neither Hadrian or I reacted to any blood which is a positive sign."

"I thought you wouldn't react badly to it," she prompted.

"We wouldn't, but we'd certainly be able to tell that it was there."

"Right." She didn't wait for him to respond before going back to the car and grabbing a couple of bottles of water and another blanket. She was just grateful that Hadrian kept his car supplied with this kind of thing. Though come to think of it, maybe there was a good reason for that. Whatever the reason, it didn't hurt to be prepared.

Before turning away, she had another thought and grabbed the box of cereal bars she'd seen bouncing around. It wouldn't do much about the malnutrition right at that moment, but it would be something to take the edge off, and that would go a long way.

She glanced in on the shifter, relieved to see she was still sleeping. While it sounded like Kamali didn't blame the two women, it was still probably better that she wasn't faced with two of her tormentors.

The moment she returned, she handed the water and snacks to the women, before draping the blanket over them.

"How long until help arrives?"

Issac shook his head. "Not soon enough."

"Where are the other two?"

He was about to respond when she got the answer for herself. Zack and Hadrian barrelled out of the building with Michael between them, straining to get free.

"Let go of me, you monsters," he screamed.

Cassie caught herself before she flinched, not wanting to give in to fear of a man she'd known for years. "He shouldn't be giving them so much trouble, should he?" she whispered to Issac.

He shook his head. "He must have done something to himself."

"With what he learned here?" She dreaded to think about what that could possibly be.

"I don't know. This isn't something I've ever seen before." He grimaced.

"We should help." She stepped forward without thinking. Two of her mates were in danger, and she needed to do something to support them. Maybe she could do something...

Michael pulled away and threw a punch at Hadrian.

"No!" Cassie shouted, sparks flying from her hands and forming a barrier between the two men.

Michael bounced back, falling to the floor and howling in pain. Cassie's eyes widened as she looked on, realising what she'd done. No magic in front of any humans. And yet that was precisely what she'd done.

He struggled to his feet, wobbling slightly as he stood before lashing out again. Her magic ripped from her once more, completely beyond her control. At this point, she wasn't sure she even cared that much. He was trying to hurt her mates, and she wasn't going to let that happen.

This time, when her magic lashed out, she harnessed it, instructing it to circle his wrists and form handcuffs made out of sparks. She breathed a sigh of relief to see him paying more attention to the bonds around him than to her mates. That was going to make subduing him a lot easier.

"Can you make a chain to tie him?" Hadrian asked.

She nodded, not ready to form words yet. It was already too late for her to stop using magic. Michael and the two women had already seen her use it. Not that it mattered anyway. They knew about paranormals or else they wouldn't be here. Instructing her magic to create a chain, she forced it to loop around the centre of his handcuffs.

"Thank you." Hadrian took the other end of the magical chain from her and secured it around the drain pipe.

He strode back to her and pulled her into his arms, dropping a kiss on the top of her head.

"What will happen to me?" she whispered.

"Nothing. You had no choice. It was do what you did, or let him hurt more people." He rocked her back and forth.

"He saw me though."

"I know. We'll deal with it," he promised.

"Hadrian..." Zack warned as the sound of approaching cars grew louder.

Cassie pulled away from the vampire's comforting embrace, ready to face the consequences of what she'd done.

The cars came to a stop, and the doors swung open. The vampire from the previous murder site stepped out, along with a petite blonde woman who reminded Cassie of a pixie she'd once met.

"What did I tell you, Hadrian?" the woman asked, sounding more exasperated than angry.

"Cassie didn't have a choice."

"Of course she didn't," the woman muttered.

"Jeanie..." the older vampire warned.

"Yes, yes, Richard. I know. It wasn't magic in front of people with no clue." She sighed and studied the man fighting against the magical chain. "This is him?"

"That's the one. There are two women who were also involved, under the blanket there. But I think they were coerced from what we learned," Hadrian responded.

"Right." Jeanie signalled for two other men to join her and strode over to the human captives.

"We'll take it from here. Do you need anything else?" Richard asked.

"We do have a casualty. A shifter. We need to take her back to the lab for some tests, then we'll be able to submit our report." Zack sounded completely different to his normal self, but she didn't question it. Not with other people around.

"Is she still alive?" Richard asked.

Cassie nodded. "Weak, but alive."

"Very well. Take her with you, but I'll be sending

someone to take a statement from her tomorrow. You're going to need everything you can to convince the High Council to let this through." He walked away before saying anything else.

"We're going to have to go in front of the High Council?" Her eyes widened as she asked, dreading to even imagine would that would be like.

"No, we just have to supply the report," Issac responded. "Now let's get home and we can do that in the morning."

"I like the sound of that." A shower and her bed sounded like a great plan. Followed by a resignation letter to the lab. Even with Michael out of the way, she didn't want to be there any more. Even if she couldn't join the rest of them as part of their team.

SIXTEEN

One week later...

She sighed and pushed the laptop away from her. No matter how many times she looked at the same thing, the results didn't change.

"What's up?" Issac asked, putting a cup of tea down and pulled up one of the other wheelie chairs to look at the various things all over her desk. While she might not officially work with them, the three of them were acting as if they did.

"When I look at our blood samples, they're still doing the same thing. I can see the minute differences in mine, Zack, and Hadrian's, but yours doesn't change at all."

"Show me?"

"Do you understand it?"

He chuckled. "No. But sometimes a fresh pair of eyes is all you need."

She sighed and turned the laptop screen to face him. "See these tiny specks here?" She pointed to them on the pictures of Hadrian and Zack's blood. "They match these ones." She pointed to the bigger ones in the image of her own blood.

"And you think that's the start of the power-sharing?" Issac asked.

"It seems logical after Zack's freak out the other day."

"Ah, yes. That." Issac smiled broadly, clearly as amused by the situation as she was. "But the mating bond starting is great news. What's the problem?"

She sighed. "This is the problem." Enlarging the image of Issac's blood sample, she filled the screen with its truth.

"I see. You think because I don't have any squiggles yet, it's going to be a problem."

"Did you just call witch magic squiggles?" She raised an eyebrow.

"Of course. What else would you like to call it?"

She couldn't believe him. He'd seen what she was capable of, it wasn't to be dismissed as mere squiggles.

"That's not the point. You not having any is..."

"Perfectly normal," he interrupted, placing his hand over hers. "I'm a death magic being, and you're a life magic one. It's going to take a little bit longer for our magic to merge. There's nothing wrong with that, I promise. But I can find another necromancer for you to talk to if you want to be sure."

"No, it's okay..." she trailed off, trying to work out how to respond. It wasn't that she didn't believe him, more that it didn't make much sense to her scientific mind. Why would life and death magic beings be able to mate if it took them longer to bond? It didn't quite make sense.

A door slammed down the corridor, and the two of them perked up.

"I didn't think they'd be back for another couple of hours?" she asked, excitement filling her voice.

"They weren't supposed to be," Issac responded. "But let's hope it's a good sign."

Hadrian and Zack entered the room moments later, though nothing on their faces revealed how their meeting with their superiors at PCI had gone. She'd thought it was a good sign that they let Issac stay behind, but it was impossible to tell with an organisation she'd never come across before.

"So?" she prompted when they didn't say anything.

"We were updated on the case. Kamali's statement was enough to convince the High Council that Michael needed to be tried as a paranormal, not a human," Hadrian answered.

"Is she okay?"

Zack nodded. "Still recovering, and she's sent a fresh blood sample for you, but by her own admission, they hadn't done much to her."

"Hmm." She only had five blood samples to go from, and none of them were particularly useful. Even so, she'd managed to come up with a theory that Michael had been trying to introduce different types of magic into paranormals. Most notably witch magic, but she figured that was just because it was one of the most recognisable.

"Anyway, the two human women have been released. After being hypnotised by Richard. He's going to have to check in on them regularly to make sure they don't remember, but it's nothing too bad.," Hadrian said.

"Michael was threatening their children," Zack added. "That's how he got them to do the work. A little digging revealed one was a nurse, and the other filled out a position like yours at the lab. There's a chance he didn't know you were a witch after all and was just hoping to use you as another worker in his dirty little plot." He sneered as he said the words, clearly unimpressed by what the man had been doing.

Cassie's hand flew to her mouth. "That's awful."

"It is. But thankfully, none of the kids were hurt. The only casualties appear to be the ones we know about."

"And there's no chance that he wasn't working alone? Maybe this was bigger than just one experimental lab," Issac suggested.

"It might be, but none of the evidence suggests that. Then again, I only know what we were told. And you know what Jeanie is like. She's never going to reveal anything she doesn't have to. Especially when we woke her up last week." Hadrian gave a weak smile. Maybe it hadn't just been Cassie's insistence that had made him wake up his boss then. Maybe there was some small, vindictive part of him that just wanted some kind of revenge.

"I suppose knowing lives were saved because of us will have to be reward enough," Cassie mused.

"Spoken like a true member of the PCI department," Hadrian joked.

"Hardly." She snorted, unable to help herself. "I'm just a lame hanger-on you're never going to be able to get rid of." While she said the words as a joke, there was an edge to them even she hadn't expected. She didn't want to be a spare part. She wanted to work with them to solve whatever case came their way.

"Is that true?" he asked, holding up what looked like a lanyard with an ID card hanging from it.

She blinked a couple of times, trying to put his words and what he was doing together. "Are you saying what I think you're saying?" she whispered the words, too scared that she might be wrong and they might not want her after all. That was how things seemed to go for her. She didn't expect today to be any different.

"Welcome to the Paranormal Criminal Investigations Department," Zack answered for him.

"More importantly, welcome to the team," Hadrian asked, handing her the badge.

She stared at the pass, unable to form words. It might have been what she wanted, but she hadn't believed it was something she'd actually get. But now she had. Now she was part of a team. The best team she could have ever imagined.

"You're not going to regret this," she promised.

"We never thought we would," Issac replied.

She didn't say anything else, just ran around and kissed each of them on the cheek. They'd already given her a desk, but this had made it official. She planned to earn her keep. She'd be an integral part of the team, offering something that the rest of them couldn't.

This meant that she wasn't just Cassie anymore. Now she was Agent Cassie Morgan of the PCI. Working with her mates to fight serious paranormal crime, and loving every minute of it.

THE END

Thank you for reading *Spell Caster*. Cassie and the team will return soon in *Spell Tamer* where they'll have a new crime to solve! For release details, you can join my Facebook Group or Mailing List. For more reverse harem set in the Paranormal Council Universe, try Saving Eira!

SPELL TAMER

Spell Tamer will be coming in 2019 and will see Cassie and the team taking on another crime to solve. Expect false accusations, growing bonds, more magic, and maybe even some steamy moments! While you're waiting – why not check out other stories set in the Paranormal Council Universe – including Blood and Deceit, a standalone featuring Richard, who you met in Spell Caster! Read on for the first chapter!

BLOOD AND DECEIT CHAPTER 1

Blood and Deceit is an urban fantasy romance with vampires and necromancers set in the Paranormal Council Universe. It can be read as a standalone.
You can check it out here:
http://books2read.com/bloodanddeceit

Tabitha breathed out in relief. The alley was completely clear of people, so there was no way she was going to get caught. Humming softly, she called upon the blood leaking from the man's open wounds. Purple smoke rose up from him and circled her own arm. Instead of using it, she directed it into a large gem hanging around her neck.

Perfect.

So long as no one ever found out. If they did...well, she wasn't all that sure what would happen. Without a Necromancer Council, there was no one to tell her what she could and couldn't do. That would mean if she ended up in front of anyone, it was going to be the High Council and given their shutting down the Necromancer Council in the first place, that wouldn't bode well for her.

Footsteps sounded at the end of the alley. She needed to get going.

Trying to stay as calm as possible, she sauntered. Nothing drew more attention than running somewhere, mainly when she'd actually done something wrong. At least she hadn't killed the man herself. As far as she could tell, that was down to a vampire, though she wouldn't put any money on it.

She slipped into the next alley, knowing it would bring her out near Potions, the latest paranormal only club to spring up in the city. It had always baffled her how the paranormal clubs were never discovered by humans. The only explanation she could think of was that a dryad or an elf was casting some kind of concealment magic. It would take a lot of their energy to do that.

"One please." She smiled sweetly at the ticket seller.

The shifter looked her up and down, no doubt trying to work out what she was. It happened all the time. Necromancers were notoriously difficult to recognise unless the person already knew one well. They also kept to themselves, meaning a lot of paranormals had never come across the death magic-wielding race.

"A fiver," he grunted.

Tabitha dug into her pocket and slid the money over to him. He grabbed it and slammed a ticket down.

"Thanks," she muttered.

Slipping through the door, she entered the club and recoiled away from the squirming masses of people on the dance floor. Turning up her nose, she sauntered over to the bar and got herself a drink. She hated bars and clubs. They always smelled of sweat and so many bodies in one room sent her vision funny with all the life force coming off them.

"You made it then," a rough voice came from behind her.

"Yes. Have you got what I asked for?"

Instead of answering, the man passed her a hotel room key. "Room one-six-five."

"How do I know this isn't a trap?"

"You don't," he replied. "You're just going to have to trust me."

She snorted. "That doesn't seem like a great option."

"Maybe not, but what you're after can't be brought into a place like this."

She scowled, not looking at the man. While he was right, it wasn't her who'd insisted they met here. In fact, she'd have preferred it if they'd encountered one another in the alley with the dead body.

"So, do you have it?"

"Here." She pulled the gem from around her neck and shoved it into his hands.

"And it's fresh?"

"Yes. From tonight."

"Thank you, Tabitha, you've been a real help."

He didn't linger any longer.

She sighed, knowing she had to get going if she was going to receive her payment. She hated having to resort to stealing life force from the recently dead but she'd lost her job when the Council disbanded and she had to make a living somehow. The fact it was probably other necromancers reaping the rewards of her misfortune wasn't lost on her either. Sometimes she wished she'd been born as something else. Shifters had it pretty damn good. No one tried to make them do things they didn't want to and, slowly but surely, they were taking over the way the whole paranormal community was being run. She wasn't even sure how they were doing that. They'd gone from a minority to the ones holding almost all the power within months.

Pushing through sweaty bodies, she made her way to the exit, cursing the people she was doing business with. She'd spent money getting in here and she hadn't even been paid for the dirty work she'd done. That wasn't good business but she really had no choice. Not when the alternative risked holding onto the contraband life energy for longer than was necessary.

Thankfully, the hotel the man had chosen was only a few doors down and she made it there in record time. Relaxing her shoulders, she walked through the door and flashed a smile at the receptionist. She needed to appear as if she was meant to be here rather than she was just making a flying visit. She'd never have chosen somewhere like here, not when the hotel room would have to be booked under a name. Too many red flags for her liking.

The elevator took forever to get to the first floor. Why were things always so slow when they shouldn't be? She needed to get to room one-six-five, get what she did this for and get out again.

She let out a breath as the doors opened, revealing a blissfully empty hallway. There'd be no hiding from life lights here at least. Not when she needed to get out of here as soon as possible. If anyone worked out the body she'd left had been drained, it would be dangerous for any necromancer in the vicinity. Never mind one who'd been alone the whole time. Knowing her luck, they'd call the new crime department they'd set up. She didn't fancy her chances against them. The human police were problem enough but could be tricked with fairly basic magic. Paranormal police? She shuddered. She just didn't want to find out.

Reaching the door she needed, she positioned the key card above the slot and readied herself for whatever she'd find on the other side of the door.

She jumped back as the door swung open, revealing a man in a bloody shirt and with a panicked look on his face.

Tabitha's eyes widened. What had she just walked into?

"We need to go," the man said, grabbing her wrist and trying to pull her down the corridor.

"I can't, I need to..." she gestured towards the room, only gaining another tug from the man.

"Trust me, there's nothing in there for you. Time to go."

The earnest look in his eyes made her pause but if she didn't get what she came for...

"It's a trap, Tabitha..."

"How do you know my name?" she demanded.

"I'll explain later. Trust me, please?"

Indecision warred within her until a crash sounded from the hotel room, making up her mind. She'd find another way to get what she needed. For now, she had to stay alive.

Hopefully, this man would help with that. If not, she was dead either way.

Thank you for reading the first chapter of Blood and Deceit! You can find the whole book here: http://books2read.com/bloodanddeceit

1. Wolf Blessed (Audiobook Available)
2. Fae Blessed (Audio Coming Soon)
3. Elf Blessed (Coming Soon)

Paranormal Criminal Investigations (paranormal mystery reverse harem)

1. Spell Caster (Coming Soon)
2. Spell Tamer (Coming Soon)
3. Spell Wielder (Coming Soon)

Stories From the Paranormal Council Universe (each story stands alone)

- Frost's Forfeit (Audio Coming Soon)
- Spells and Curses
- Death's Choice (Audio Coming Soon)
- Stories From the Paranormal Council Universe Collection (includes His Lost Bear, Spellbound, Under Her Spell, Catching His Ladybird, Snakes and Ladders, and Falling Ashes) (Audio Coming Soon)
- Blood & Deceit

OTHER BOOKS BY LAURA GREENWOOD

Ashryn Barker Trilogy (urban fantasy, completed series)

1. Shattered Illusions (Audiobook Available)
2. Broken Illusions (Audiobook Available)
3. Tarnished Illusions (Audio Coming Soon)

- The Ashryn Barker Trilogy Boxed Set

Forgotten Gods World (paranormal/mythology romance)

- Protectors of Poison (Zodiac Shifters) (Audio Coming Soon)

The Afterlife Journeys (fantasy romance)

1. Reaper (Audiobook Available)
2. Fallen (Coming Soon)

Untold Tales (urban fantasy fairy tales)

- Golden Wings (coming soon)

1. Balanced Scales

ME Contemporary Standalones (contemporary romance)

1. Sweet About Me (Audiobook Available)
2. Kneel For Me (Audiobook Available)
3. Heard From Me (Audiobook Available)

4. Laid By Me
5. Con With Me (Coming Soon)

- If The Shoe Fits (Audio Coming Soon)

Rats: Tori (steampunk reverse harem, completed series)

1. Ruler of Rats
2. Collector of Rats
3. Yuletide of Rats

Standalones

- Hidden (dystopian)

Co-Written Books

Twin Souls Trilogy, co-written with Arizona Tape (paranormal romance, completed series)

1. Soulshift
2. Soulswap
3. Soultrade

Dragon Soul Series, co-written with Arizona Tape (paranormal)

1. Torn Soul (Audio Coming Soon)
2. Bound Soul
3. Stray Soul (Coming Soon)

The Renegade Dragons Series, co-written with Arizona Tape (paranormal)

1. Fifth Soul (Audiobook Available)

2. Fifth Round

Seven Wardens, co-written with Skye MacKinnon
(paranormal/fantasy reverse harem)

1. From the Deeps (Audiobook Available)
2. Into the Mists
3. Beneath the Earth
4. Within the Flames
5. Above the Waves
6. Under the Ice
7. TBC

- Beyond the Loch (Coming Soon, series prequel)
- Through the Storms (to be read between From
  the Deeps & Into the Mists)
- Below the Baubles (to be read between Above
  the Waves & Under the Ice)
- Seven Wardens Boxed Set: Books 1-4

Harem of Misery, co-written with A.K. Koonce (paranormal
reverse harem)

1. Pandora's Pain
2. Pandora's Envy (Coming Soon)

Standalones

- Ocean's Serenade (co-written with J&L Wells.
  Paranormal Romance)
- Valentine Pride (co-written with L.A. Boruff.
  Paranormal Romance. Coming Soon)

Available Audiobooks

Further information can be found here:
www.authorlauragreenwood.co.uk/p/audio.html

Fated Seasons: Spring:

1. Chasing Aledwen

Fated Seasons: Winter

1. Saving Eira

Blessed

1. Wolf Blessed
2. Fae Blessed

The Afterlife Journeys

1. Reaper

The Paranormal Council

1. The Dryad's Pawprint
2. The Vixen's Bark (in production)

Ashryn Barker Trilogy

1. Shattered Illusions
2. Broken Illusions
3. Tarnished Illusions

Thornheart Coven

1. Witch's Potion
2. Witch's Spark

ME Series

1. Sweet About Me
2. Kneel For Me
3. Heard From Me

- If The Shoe Fits (in production)

Dragon Soul, co-written with Arizona Tape

1. Torn Soul (in production)

The Renegade Dragons, co-written with Arizona Tape

1. Fifth Soul

From the Deeps, co-written with Skye MacKinnon

1. From the Deeps
2. Into the Mists (in production)

Standalone Stories From The Paranormal Council Universe

- Frost's Forfeit (in production)
- Death's Choice (in production)
- Stories From the Paranormal Council Universe (in production)

Forgotten Gods

- Protectors of Poison

ABOUT LAURA GREENWOOD

Laura is a USA Today Bestselling Author of paranormal and fantasy romance. When she's not writing, she can be found drinking ridiculous amounts of tea, trying to resist French Macaroons, and watching the Pitch Perfect trilogy for the hundredth time (at least!)

Follow the Author:

Website: www.authorlauragreenwood.co.uk
Mailing List: www.authorlauragreenwood.co.uk/p/mailing-list-sign-up.html
Facebook Group:
http://facebook.com/groups/theparanormalcouncil
Facebook Page:
http://facebook.com/authorlauragreenwood
Bookbub: www.bookbub.com/authors/laura-greenwood
Instagram: www.instagram.com/authorlauragreenwood
Twitter: www.twitter.com/lauramg_tdir

Printed in Poland
by Amazon Fulfillment
Poland Sp. z o.o., Wrocław